The French Perfumer

EUROPEAN TYCOONS
BOOK TWO

LEANNE LOVEGROVE

Copyright © 2024 by Leanne Lovegrove

All rights reserved.

No part of this book may be reproduced in any form or by any electronic or mechanical means, including information storage and retrieval systems, without written permission from the author, except for the use of brief quotations in a book review.

Dedication

*To the perfumes of Grasse and the people who make them, this story
was inspired by you.*

K itty, I'm sorry I can't do it. Please forgive me. I don't love you and can't marry you today, Stuart x

Chapter One

Kitty Landers buried her face in the silky-smooth fabric of the pale pink wedding dress she carried. Bunching the frock up to her face, she inhaled deeply before closing her eyes. Damn that scent. The scent that clung to the dress had the power to enrapture and transport her. Back home, back to him, to happier times. The fragrance was from *Montgomery Perfumes* and it had once been her favourite. Now, the floral undertones and the light magnolia notes turned her stomach.

It was a perfume she never wanted to smell again.

Kitty's eyes popped open. She lifted her head from the gown, squared her shoulders, held the heavy layers of her wedding dress aloft for a few more seconds before dropping it, with great ceremony, into the rubbish. It crumpled, one perfect frill of the hem overlapping the lip of the bin that sat on the congested train platform.

Even then she couldn't tear her gaze away from the discarded and crushed fabric. She could do this and was doing the right thing; dumping the dress would allow her to move on. It was the first step in accepting that she'd been jilted at the altar. And let's face it, what would she do with an unwanted wedding gown anyway? With a deep sigh, she inhaled again keen to be rid of the lingering aroma of the perfume. Instead, she welcomed the unpleasant reek of oil, fuel and cigarette smoke as she stood on the noisy platform in Grasse.

The French station bustled with Friday afternoon commuters heading to destinations for the weekend ahead. No one paid any attention to the crazy woman who'd just chucked her wedding dress in the bin. They were not like her fellow passengers on the plane from Brisbane to Singapore. They hadn't ignored her as she sat in economy wearing the gown. By the time she arrived at Changi airport, some semblance of sense had returned, and she realised how ridiculous she must have appeared in her full wedding attire, tiara still atop her head. But even then, she couldn't dispose of it, not yet, and she'd nursed that dress with its folds and pleats like a new-born baby on her lap all the way to Charles de Gaulle Airport, ignoring the silent stares and sympathetic looks from others on her international flight.

But now, finally, she'd arrived at her destination of the hinterland town of Grasse in the southeast of France. Her arrival in the perfume capital of the world heralded a chance to start over and rebuild her shattered life.

Time to get started. Except her feet didn't cooperate. Instinct had her wanting to give the elegant pink gown one last glance, a final look at the lace overlay and diamante studs across the bust that resembled the night-time stars.

No. She refused to be lost to nostalgia; for what was, what

should have been. Kitty turned away from the rubbish bin and searched for her red suitcase.

She took one step, then another towards her new life and reached for the worn handle of her luggage. Long, slender fingers connected with hers and fought for space on the leather grip. The fingers belonged to a masculine hand with smooth skin and neat, square nails and a tiny bunching of hair at each knuckle. They were impressive hands but... the scent! It was a distinct fragrance that didn't drift slowly towards her, it slammed into her and immobilised her on the spot. Blanketed in the most divine aroma, Kitty clutched the handle tighter.

For the second time in minutes, the train station disappeared as she travelled on a sensory experience. But this journey was different. Again, the noise surrounding her receded as she focused on the strong musk with cedarwood and hints of cinnamon and lemon and perhaps sage? It was woody and divine...and beautiful.

This scent belonged to *someone.* A man who always got served first in line or was the last to arrive at a party but the most welcome. It was bold and enticing and...

The case jerked and the fingers gripping hers tried to dislodge her hand. Kitty was pulled from her reverie and she crashed back down to the train station with a thump, the sounds drumming in her ears once more.

The dark-haired man in front of her wore a frown to match his navy well-cut suit. His stubble was three days past a shave but illuminated turquoise eyes staring intently in her direction. Eyes the colour of the water sluicing gently back and forth on the sandy beaches in the nearby Cote d'Azur. But of course, she hadn't experienced that, only briefly glimpsing the brochures and dreaming, hoping that one day she would see it. Perhaps, now, she didn't need to.

The man's chest rose and fell as if he were drawing in the bouquet of smells, too. Was he inhaling her scent? Uncertain, she dropped her hand, and the suitcase held fast in his grip. She hadn't showered in over twenty-four hours and worried she reeked of plane travel and sweat, but luckily all she detected on her skin was bloody magnolia.

Kitty stepped back, bumping into a passer-by but creating space between her and the very handsome Frenchman.

He continued to stare as she stood her ground. Crease lines formed a deeper frown on his forehead.

'*Excusez-moi, je pense que vous vous trompez, ce sont nos bagages.*' As he rattled on in rapid-fire French, a woman approached from his left and placed her hand on his arm. He paused, listened to the softly spoken words, and then gazed down to the case she held, similar but clearly different from the one he grasped.

The Frenchman put down Kitty's case and looked at her, the corners of his lips barely lifting in an apologetic half-smile. '*Pardon. Je suis vraiment desole.*'

Oh, la. That accent. After all, she was in France. He could have been yelling obscenities at her and she'd have melted under the intonation of those words. One minute ago, he probably was directing impolite phrases at her. How could one language sound so sublime and as if every word was erotic and sensual?

She pondered that thought briefly before a train blasted its horn and people raced towards carriages waving to loved ones before boarding.

The Frenchman took the case off the woman and held it up

in explanation. He stepped forward, his lips parted, ready to speak, but paused, considered her intently and took a deep breath. Kitty was sure he inhaled again before the woman tugged his sleeve impatiently. With one last glance at Kitty, they moved away.

Her body sagged a little. A nice accent, damn fine-looking and a divine scent all in one package. That guy fitted the descriptive phrase: tall, dark and handsome. The only lightness was the blue of his eyes. The rest of him was dark: his dress, hair, his aura, even his scent had moody undertones. And the saunter and dominating presence as he walked away! The crowds parted as he walked through.

And on his arm was a beautiful woman who teetered in stiletto heels, carried a large designer handbag and wore a red scarf! Her skirt was pencil-thin so that it only permitted tiny steps forward, and her blouse was one of those silk, off-white blow-in-the-breeze sorts that accentuated her rose pink cheeks.

The cliché of French people being beautiful was real. These two could have graced the pages of a glossy women's fashion magazine. Kitty glanced after them but they were lost to the crowd.

Kitty's heart shattered into million pieces. Again.

Clearly, she had landed in the country of love. Well, Paris was the city of love where deliriously happy and loved-up couples kissed on every street corner. Self-preservation had kicked in she'd skedaddled out of the capital city quick smart.

At least her encounter with the gorgeous French couple had made her forget about dropping her expensive and beautiful wedding dress in the rubbish. *C'est la vie.*

She puffed air into her cheeks and picked up her case along

with her self-esteem and determination. The small slip of paper she held in her left fist was her first step on the road to recovery. With a flick of her wrist, she read the address again, the location meant nothing to her but she'd find it.

Pierre Joubert opened the car door for Ms Melodie Dubois. Her perfume was pleasant but non-distinct. If one wore a fragrance, it had to make a statement and not blend into the wearer or the environment. This scent was too subtle.

He could not get the scent of the woman at the train station out of his head. It had been different: floral, yes, magnolia certainly, but it stood out and was immediately discernible. He'd had to control himself from moving in close to her neck and running his nose along her skin.

But he hadn't needed to. A quality perfume lasted. And hers had; he knew it had been applied hours before and still lingered. It was not a local perfume and had piqued his interest. But it wasn't a product of the *House of Joubert*. His family company produced the best perfumes not only in Grasse but in the world. That scent might have been interesting, but it wasn't in their league.

Ms Dubois exited the Bentley. They'd arrived at the children's home and stood before *Maison de Roses*. Like most local buildings, the grand three-storey home was constructed of stone, and over time, age had covered some bricks in mildew, others in wild grass. To a newcomer it might appear foreboding but that was only the stately architecture. The interior was warm and welcoming; he'd made sure of that.

Pierre hoped the new schoolteacher had packed more sensible clothing as he watched her step forward, struggling to move in her tight skirt. Ms Dubois might be the most skilled tutor he could secure but if she wasn't prepared to get dirty, come down to the children's level and play with them each day, it wasn't going to work. Not for these children. This wasn't a traditional school where obedient students sat reciting times tables or completing their homework on command. These were good kids who deserved the best and he hoped Ms Dubois would deliver.

'Papa Pierre!' Claude raced outside and wrapped his arms around Pierre's hips. He patted the boy on the back as his heart swelled with pride; Claude was special and reminded him of his brother at the same age. People thought of Pierre as a ruthless businessman who was pragmatic and devoid of emotion, and perhaps he was all those things, but every time he saw these children, he came alive. They gave him purpose.

'*Bonjour, Claude.*'

The boy gazed at him with adoration in his eyes. 'This is Ms Dubois and she's going to help you with your French and mathematics.'

The boy's grin dipped. Like many of the kids, Claude struggled to read and write and would prefer to be running around playing in the spacious garden instead.

Pierre gestured with his chin and the boy knew he was to address their guest. Obediently he held out his hand to greet her. In response, Melodie sank to her knees and addressed Claude directly. Pierre watched as the child became putty in her hands.

His shoulders dropped with relief.

'If you help me show Ms Dubois around, I'll have time for a quick game of football before I head back to the office.'

Claude squealed and reached for both of their hands and propelled them forward through the heavy, solid timber entrance.

Other than his flower farm, Rose House was the only other place Pierre felt anything remotely like contentment. His flowers were his selfish indulgence and passion and, by extension, his work, but here, this was the real world. These children had nothing and no one, and he worked very hard to ensure they were loved.

As he entered the dim and cool interior, a weight bore down upon his shoulders and a heaviness returned to his limbs. Rose House always made him think of his brother.

Chapter Two

Halfway up one of the many steep hills of Grasse, Kitty paused to catch her breath. She was daydreaming of a sexy French man walking beside her while wheeling her luggage and teasing her with his smile and exotic accent. Other visitors to the town would be admiring the rolling hills and buildings leaning into the landscape. Not Kitty Landers. It was always about love. Or the sentiment of it, anyway.

There was always time to indulge in the scents around her, though. Grasse sort of smelled like home, yet also nothing like the Sunshine Coast of Australia. There she could hear the crash of waves against the shore and the smell of salt always permeated the air. Here, there was a hint of the sea, a touch in amongst a collection of other aromas. The salt surprised her because Grasse was some distance from the coast. She'd Googled the town on the train from Paris. But there were other scents too: jasmine, but also mimosa, orange blossom and lavender. Funny, she would have expected the divine, yet subtle, fragrance of roses.

Kitty searched her surroundings for the source of the intense fragrances. The hills enveloping Grasse housed flower farms of many varieties and all for one purpose: to produce perfume. Standing on the crest of the hill, she couldn't see any farms, but she wasn't far from the town centre where houses and guest hotels lined the streets.

Realisation struck and her foot collided with the corner of her suitcase as she lost concentration. Ouch! Kitty rubbed her toe in her open-sandal shoe as she gazed around her. Being here in the home of perfume was both bittersweet and overwhelming. Tears pricked at the corners of her eyes but she refused to give them purchase. Shaking her head to whisk those water droplets away on the wind, she held up the brochure.

Villa des Fleurs, the villa or house of flowers. That had to be a sign; she was meant to stay there and study the science of perfume-making in this small, French village. A world away from her life in Australia and the disaster she'd left behind.

The flyer directed her to a villa at the top of the rise. She huffed out a sigh and kept walking a few more metres until she arrived at a wrought iron gate twice her height. Kitty pushed and it swung open to reveal a path leading to a double-storey stone house. The desert colourings, surrounding greenery against a clear, cloudless sky gave it a provincial feel. Relief swept through her. She'd made it; travelled across the world to here. It was time to achieve greatness.

Stepping though the entrance, the echo of voices, soft music and the clink of glasses reached her. The reception desk was empty so she dumped her case and continued inside. She entered a large, spacious, country-style kitchen, where a group of people sat at a well-worn timber table.

'*Bonjour*,' she managed.

Heads turned in her direction. '*Ah, hallo, ma cherie*,' an older woman replied.

'I've come about a room?' she queried in English; not confident she could pull that phrase off in her rudimentary French. Without hesitation, the woman replied in English. 'Welcome, welcome. We thought everyone had arrived already. You did not arrive with the others?'

Confusion must have been obvious in her slow reply and tilt of her head. 'Um...the others?'

'You study at the Institute of Perfumery, *oui*?' she quizzed. A man came and stood beside her, a hand to the woman's waist.

'Yes, *oui*,' Kitty answered. 'I'm in the right place?'

'*C'est oui*, of course. Come in.' The woman replied but the man spoke quickly in French and gesticulated with his free hand. When he took a breath, he laughed, throwing his head back and placed his two hands to the sides of the woman's face and kissed her on the lips.

Here we go again. Kitty resigned herself to an intimate display of affection; it was almost funny. She was the perennial lover of love, and now, at her lowest, at a time when she loathed love and wished it didn't exist, love surrounded her everywhere. Nonetheless, her heart betrayed her resolve to be indifferent to such affection and did a peculiar little skipping beat as if she was envious. And she wasn't.

The kiss went on for longer than was comfortable so Kitty looked around the kitchen. The wide and open space exuded warmth. The extraordinary afternoon light shone through open doors and hatch windows onto the stone floor with bright white cabinets. Fresh flowers sat on benches; Kitty knew each variety.

The group sitting at the table had recommenced their conversations and were speaking English. Excellent! Even though her goal was to improve her French, English was so much easier.

On the table a collection of glasses filled with both red and white wine sat beside platters of cheeses. Her stomach rumbled; she'd last eaten a snack on the train hours ago.

A hand touched her shoulder and she zoned back in.

'I'm Adrienne, your host and that is my husband, Raphael, or Raph for short.' She pointed to the man leaving the kitchen. 'Welcome to *Villa des Fleurs*. We're very excited to have you stay.'

'My name is Katherine but everyone calls me Kitty.'

'And where are you from, Kitty?'

'Australia.'

'Oh, *Australie*, such a long way. Please sit, sit.' Adrienne ushered her to a chair and with her head tilted to the side, she pointed to the wine bottles.

'White, please.' Kitty sat.

'Hello! Are you starting the course next week, too?' the man next to her asked in a strong, American drawl.

'Um, yes. Everyone doing the course stays here, right? That's what the brochure said.' She removed it from her pocket and held it up.

'Yeah, sure. Hey guys, this here is...' He looked to her with raised eyebrows.

'Kitty.'

'Kitty, from...'

'Australia.'

'Wow, Australia.'

The group erupted in greetings. A woman across the table spoke in broken English. 'I didn't realise Australia had a perfume market. It must be small. What experience do you have?'

Okay.

The woman's dark hair matched her midnight eyes as she stared at Kitty waiting for a reply. She had an accent Kitty didn't recognise but perhaps might be Italian.

'Um, no, they do. I'm from Queensland and I worked at the largest and most successful perfume manufacturer in Australia.' Was it? Kitty wasn't sure but it sounded impressive.

'Really?' Another man down the end of the table muttered as he ate a slice of prosciutto.

'Yes,' she replied with confidence. Not that she wanted to advocate for *Montgomery Perfumes*, but they had been a good employer. Their son simply hadn't been a good fiancé. 'Their fragrances are floral based...'

'All perfumes originate from flowers.' The most gorgeous woman Kitty had ever laid eyes upon, spoke. She leaned her head on her hand as though she could hardly be bothered to stay awake. Like most of the people at the table, her hair was dark, but hers was shoulder length and curled inwards at the base. In contrast to her dark features, large silver hoop earrings almost touched her shoulders. She reminded Kitty of Juliette Binoche out of the movie, *Chocolat*. She loved that movie. Except this woman didn't look all sweetness and light like that main character. But she *was* French.

'Yeah, of course.' Kitty spluttered in reply. She knew that...

'So, what are your qualifications?' The second American man seated to her left, bulged out of a white T-shirt sporting a large star-spangled flag. At least the Americans were easy to spot.

Kitty bought time by nibbling some cheese, chewing on a cracker and sipping her wine. 'Qualifications?'

'Yeah. Did you major in chemistry or science and have you studied perfume before?'

The wine she'd just drunk burned her chest like acid.

'Well, I learned on the job.'

A heavy blanket of silence descended on the group before the room erupted and they talked over each other sometimes reverting to their native tongues.

'My background is chemical engineering, so I'm going to romp this in.' The only other blonde in the room said this in a perfect English accent. How had she not noticed her already?

The occupants of the table then proceeded to announce their degrees and experience, leaving Kitty to listen and develop a thick layer of self-doubt. Zoning out, she gulped the last remnants of her wine, stood and slunk from the table. The group didn't even catch their breath and kept rattling on, not noticing her exit.

Standing outside on the terrace, she released a sigh. It was early evening and the sun was a faded orange orb in the sky, sinking slowly towards the horizon. An apricot haze blanketed the town sprawled out below. It must have been about twenty degrees, but her bare arms and legs clad in T-shirt and denim shorts, erupted in goose pimples. Kitty rubbed her arms.

'It's beautiful, yes?' Adrienne appeared by her side.

Kitty soaked up the majestic view. 'Yes, stunning. I've never been anywhere like it.'

'Have you travelled from Australia before?'

Kitty shook her head.

'It must be a shock.' Adrienne patted her on the arm like a caring aunt. *Chérie,* we don't have a booking for you, but no trouble, if you are studying at the Institute, we will always make room for you. It's important to study with the other students and travel to your course together each day.'

That thought filled her with dread.

'I'll show you your room. You ready?'

Kitty agreed and was led back into the villa and up a flight of stairs. A long narrow corridor housed rooms on each side. Stopping outside one door, Adrienne unlocked it and let her pass through the open door first. Like everything here, it was roomy and in the same desert colours of tangerine and muted yellows and oranges. 'It's lovely. Thank you.'

Adrienne kissed her on both cheeks and left. Kitty glimpsed her suitcase in the corner and was grateful it had been delivered up the stairs; then she collapsed onto the bed.

Chapter Three

Kitty woke with a start, groggy and out of sorts. She freshened up, dressed, and then rushed downstairs to discover the villa empty, the kitchen table strewn with the detritus of breakfast. No surprise her classmates had left without her. A croissant sat alone on a plate; she swiped it and bit into as she hurried down the hill.

'Bloody jetlag!' she cursed as she reached the town centre and tried to locate the Institute of Perfumery.

Her frantic search lasted only minutes when she spotted an impressive building of lemon-yellow bricks with white Tuscan shutters and matching white trim with a sign displaying the name of the school. At the entrance, she paused to catch her breath and calm her raging nerves. The glass doors slid open and welcomed her inside. The white theme continued in the foyer with marble columns flecked with grey and black, and a white checked tiled floor. It was grand. But there was no time to admire the architecture and interior design.

A tall and lanky man with short slicked-back hair was busy behind the counter and didn't notice her arrival.

'*Bonjour, monsieur.*'

His head remained downturned, in concentration, writing something onto a notepad.

Surreptitiously, Kitty smoothed down any wayward strands of hair, wiped her palms down her front and tried to regain more equilibrium.

'*Excusez-moi, monsieur.*' She tried again but the man didn't acknowledge her. Then she spoke in English. In her bamboozled state there was no way she could carry out this conversation in French. 'I'm so sorry I'm late, I'm here to enrol in the course.'

That caught his attention. 'I'm sorry?' His eyebrows knitted together.

'The course starting on Monday. I'd like to enrol.'

'Are you sure you're in the right place, mademoiselle?' Speaking English made his intonation sound clipped.

'Yes, I'm sure. I'd like to be a *parfumeur.*' She smiled and added an embellished French accent.

'A *parfumeuse,* I presume, given you are a woman.'

Huh! Finally, she'd met a Frenchman who didn't make her swoon. If the situation wasn't so dire, she might have found that funny. Even with the language barrier, Kitty knew she was being mocked, so she waited for more from the man currently holding her life in the balance. But he didn't assist. She'd try a different tact.

'Can you please assist me to enrol?'

He shook his head. '*Non. Je suis désolé.* I'm afraid not. Our courses are booked out months in advance. There are no vacancies until, let me see...' He made an exaggerated movement of flipping the pages in a paper diary in front of him. '...until two years' time.'

It was as if he'd sucker-punched her.

'But I've travelled from Australia to study the art of perfume making. I need to be on this course.'

'And have you studied previously?'

'Um, yes, I did a few years of hotel management.' Language wasn't required for her to work out what he thought about that.

'Studies in *chemistry*,' his accent accentuated the word, 'or science or previous perfumeries?'

'No.'

He tsked and shrugged.

Who knew the French could be so blasé?

'We cannot help you. We are a serious school and only accept the best of candidates with many years of prior experience to study the craft of perfume making.'

Years? Had she overestimated this perfume gig? It hadn't looked that difficult on the few occasions she'd been allowed in the lab at Montgomery Perfumes. Admittedly, those times had been fleeting, but not by choice. She'd have killed to be out the back mixing elements and ingredients to achieve the perfectly balanced perfume. There was only so much she could learn on the shop floor.

'I've been working for Montgomery Perfumes in Australia. They said I'm very sensitive to smell.'

With his eyes diverted, there was an upturned curl of his lips and a wrinkle of his nose. Pity was the worst! She'd have to pull up stumps. But she couldn't...wouldn't give up.

'There is another place.' His mouth twisted in distaste. 'In town, for hobbyists. You could try them.'

'Yes, thank you, okay. Where are they?' A burst of hope sprouted.

He gave her brief directions and resumed writing; she was dismissed.

Before she'd had a chance to move away from the counter, a group of people entered the foyer.

'Kitty!' Her stomach plummeted. Not wanting to, Kitty turned to face Chad and the other students from the guest-house. 'You've missed the start of the tour.'

Kitty died a little inside. She would be the laughingstock when she returned to their accommodation tonight. They already thought the Australian was a joke with no experience or qualifications. She'd worry about that later; she plastered a confident and broad smile on her face. 'I'll catch you up!' she waved as the remainder of the group cut through the entrance to another room. Kitty saw test tubes and glass wracks and high benches with stools...and then the door slammed shut. This group would be learning the serious art of how to make beautiful perfume. She dragged her feet as she trudged outside. The day had dawned into brightness and Kitty squinted. Heat permeated off the coloured pathways of the town and provided welcome warmth. People milled about in cafés and coffee shops enjoying the sunny Saturday morning. The nutty, dark roasted smell of espresso coffee floated in the air.

She craved a hit of caffeine but needed to sort out her studies first. And her life.

Based on the man's instructions, she walked further down the hill into the lower part of town.

Before long she spied a green hanging sign that welcomed her to *Ecole du Beau Parfum* - School of Beautiful Perfume.

That brought the first smile to her face today. Sure, the sign was faded to a barely-there pale green, and hung askew, and the building housed cracks along its façade. It looked so old and worn out in the midday sun she couldn't quite tell what colour it might have once been.

It could have been the most dilapidated building in the town and Kitty would still have entered. What choice did she have? The tinkle of a bell sounded as she pushed the door open.

Unlike the entry to the Institute, this office was cramped and dark with little natural light, but she could make out the desk in the corner. A black and white cat wandered along the window ledge before disappearing out of sight. A head with the most gorgeous red curls and matching impish grin popped up.

'*Bonjour et bienvenue*! How can we assist you, love?'

'I wish to become a perfumer.' Kitty uttered the words tentatively. Would this woman ridicule her, too?

'*Ah, oui, bien sur*!' The receptionist scrambled to give Kitty some brochures before scanning her computer. Kitty held her breath waiting for the interrogation about her qualifications and experience, but they didn't come. She ignored the pang that hit her in the gut that this might not be the real deal.

The bell over the door rang again and another person entered. Kitty had her head buried in completing the forms but a distinct scent became immediately obvious in the small office space. She paused taking it in before flourishing her signature across the enrolment forms and handing over her credit card.

Then she look up. *Oh, la.* Those might be her new, favourite French words. They rolled so easily off the tongue.

A man with large, dark and serious eyes observed her through thick-rimmed glasses. Despite the warm weather, he wore a collared shirt that accentuated his long and lean neck and chiselled chin and smooth jawline. His thin lips didn't offer a smile but held firm with an arrogant twist. He lifted her left hand to his lips and kissed it, all the while maintaining eye contact before speaking French words that she didn't understand. Before she blinked, he was gone leaving behind his cologne.

The fragrance was strong, heady. Kitty covered her nose and mouth to avoid being overpowered by it. It didn't work. But still, like any scent, she was transported. This time to her mother's old, colonial house. To Saturday afternoons on the verandah drinking green tea. Her mother would be busy berating Kitty's father and reciting his character flaws.

The memory of those afternoons were not happy ones. Even to this day, she didn't like green tea. Nor its smell.

The fragrance reminded her of that herbal tea but with undertones of earth and musk. Despite the man's dazzling good looks, he'd applied his cologne with a heavy hand.

The lovely receptionist brought her back to the present and handed her the information she needed for her course and wished her a *bonne journée.*

Back outside, the street was an explosion of noise and colour. Now that Kitty was enrolled in her studies, she could relax and enjoy herself until the course started on Monday. Thank goodness things had worked out. She released a big sigh.

The echo of her father's voice rattled around in her head–not that she'd spoken to him since her abandoned wedding–but she knew what he'd say. Her father would express his disappointment at her lack of organisation and her poor research skills. Hadn't she investigated each of the courses available, spoken with them, compared their fees and services? Checked dates of enrolment?

Well, hell no, she hadn't. Kitty had been too busy fleeing the country alone after being dumped by text message on the day of her wedding! And right now, she was supposed to be on her honeymoon in Paris acting loved up and fitting in perfectly in this country that oozed *l'amour*. She could barely think about it lest a tsunami of shame washed over her.

So, sorry, Dad, there hadn't been time for any of that. Bugger him and his lectures. Bugger Stuart, too. Kitty stood taller, shoulders high. Without any of the appropriate preparation, she had pulled it off. Kitty Landers was studying the art of perfume making in Grasse. That deserved celebration. Perhaps with some food? Sightseeing?

Luckily there were many options. Too many, and her mind assessed the possibilities before she chose the busiest and closest café with green umbrellas and seats lining the footpath.

Kitty followed another tourist into the venue and watched them order at the counter before finding a seat. She smiled when it was her turn and ordered *un café au lait* and a mouth-watering ham and cheese baguette.

After locating a free seat in the corner of the front courtyard, she unwrapped her food and devoured it. Crowds rushed past and even though early in May wasn't officially tourist season, tourists nursed cameras around their necks while locals pulled shopping carts of fresh produce. A large group of women wandered past carrying identical pink and gold gift bags.

Intrigued, Kitty searched the direction of where they'd come and spotted a striking pink building. It was a sign, it had to be. She loved pink, she loved pretty and it was calling her. It didn't matter what that place was or what it sold, she had it in her sights. Hunger sated and feeling more normal, she followed the crowd. She was good at that, too.

On the short incline towards pink heaven, she passed more happy shoppers all emanating from the grandiose, pink palace. It stood at the peak of the rise amongst the tangerine, melon and pale lemon buildings of the village. At the base of its grand staircase, a large white sign welcomed her to *House of Joubert* with a little bottle of *eau de perfum* painted next to the words.

A perfume factory! Things were working in her favour for the first time since she'd arrived in this foreign land. Kitty skipped up the stairs and entered a shop. Wow! The interior popped with colour and ... the smell. Her senses were overwhelmed, both visually and sensually with hundreds of competing scents. It reminded her of the factory at home. Except these were new, different aromas and she wanted to know each of them intimately.

There were perfume bottles with distinct gold and pink lining the many shelves. Kitty had surely died and gone to heaven. She pounced upon the first in a long row. Picking up the bottle, it slipped through her fingers but she caught it and clutched it to her chest. With her heart hammering fast, she checked the price tag.

Oh! With delicate fingers she placed it back down onto the shelf. Thank goodness she hadn't dropped it. Perfume was expensive in Europe and having to purchase this one bottle would seriously dent her savings.

Every other eager tourist didn't seem to mind. They snatched up bottle after bottle of the many options available. Her fingers reached out once more and traced up and down the smooth surface of one them. Oh, but to buy one ... she really would be in heaven to own such a divine fragrance. Off to the side was a square block of rose soap. That might be more affordable.

Her gaze paused on a couple. The man was captivated by his wife choosing a scent. She had tester cards held in a fan-like shape in her hand and with eyes closed, she sniffed. The man beamed in her direction, his eyes sparkling with such a look of love that Kitty's heart turned to liquid in her chest. Damn it! She'd hoped that having her own heartbroken might have cured her of her unrelenting romanticism.

Would this man leave this woman in the lurch, too? Kitty couldn't imagine that anyone who adored each other like these two clearly did, could ever be capable of such a thing.

But she'd never thought Stuart capable of that either.

Yep, now she was a cynic. Perhaps she was cured.

A woman wearing a bright, pink tee strode into the room and announced that a perfume-making class was commencing shortly and interested persons should purchase their ticket.

Oh! Kitty scanned the placards above the counter. Museum. Shop. Factory. Classes. This place had everything.

She should come back; she had plenty of time... instead, she joined the queue for the three-hour workshop and shuffled into a clinical, white room.

Chapter Four

Tart. Strong. Astringent. Kitty identified the smells. Sweet. Indulgent. Comforting. Lemon connoted vanilla, cinnamon and sugar which this time transported her to afternoon tea with her grandmother with baked citrus tarts straight from the oven.

Kitty closed her eyes as she smelled the baking, her grandmother's talcum powder and the mustiness of her front room. Kitty could taste the amazing sugary goodness of the treat with its flaky pastry base and the filling that was creamy and tangy and to-die-for. Her body flooded with warmth of the memories of a time she was happy and loved.

Their teacher in the perfume workshop reminisced of childhood lemon sweets bought from the local corner shop that she'd savour for hours at a time. Another member of the class mentioned cleaning products. There were many cooking memories and recollections of family traditions.

Getting to the heart of an essence was the purpose of the

lesson. As a group they repeated this process with ten fragrances. Each vial evoked vivid memories of times past, both pleasant and disagreeable, but always memorable. Each smell meant something different to each student. As a young woman who'd worn feminine scents, Kitty knew choosing the right fragrance was important. What she'd not realised was that perfume was a relationship, a commitment, became part of who you were and what you represented when you wore it. As the retail assistant at Montgomery's, she'd acted on instinct when helping customers choose their perfect scent.

Now she understood, essences were so much more than a nice odour and Kitty wanted to learn how to craft them, not sell them. It was her time to create.

At least the disaster that had become her life had allowed this opportunity. No point dwelling on it, but she wondered if she and Stuart had married, would she still be wiping down counters, restocking shelves and greeting customers? Her desired career trajectory had been well vocalised and sometimes scoffed at by his family. Promises had been made but never acted upon.

Kitty shook off the past; her time was now. She was eager to get started and danced on her tiptoes. Ideas had been bubbling in her brain for months, hell, years.

In front of each student were small black bottles with a dozen or so plastic pipettes, narrow strips of card and glass beakers. The scene mirrored a science laboratory by being clinical, clean and stark-white. Where was the colour inspiration? She declared the lab uninspiring but it wasn't about where they stood, it was about what they created.

Kitty inhaled the scent at the base of the strip again. She could drown herself in these aromas.

With her clipped and exotic accent, the '*nez*' or nose as those in the industry were called, asked them to conjure an image of a place or time that would become their perfume. What would be its theme? Its genesis? The idea behind it?

Kitty was learning more in this class than she had in the last five years. It was a practical step-by-step guide. And she knew what she wanted to create: home. Home was the sun, sultry heat, salty sea air, the beach and the freshness unique to Queensland. But while she might have her idea, how the hell was she going to make a scent smell like that?

Olfactory, top notes, heart notes and base notes. Yes, she'd heard of these elements. She knew the essences but didn't know how to blend them to match what was in her head.

She reached for patchouli. It was from the natural environment and could form her base note, be the lasting essence as it was stronger and more potent. Their teacher lectured in her kind and nurturing voice that should have carried Kitty along. Somehow, though, with these bottles and the choices in front of her, her creativity dissolved like flat lemonade. Where was her passion hiding? Like a racehorse, she'd frozen at the gate. Without sufficient consideration or concentration, she blended a mixture of the essential oils hoping it would work in the end.

The teacher glided around the room, inhaling the perfumes with dramatic effect. Kitty noticed on some she went quiet, others she exclaimed their brilliance and natural ability. Inside her tummy muscles clenched, hoping the *nez* wouldn't make her way to Kitty at the far back of the room. No such luck.

'*Bonjour, mademoiselle,*' the teacher said brightly and sprayed a dot of Kitty's fragrance onto a spare white card and raised it to her nose before...she coughed and covered her mouth. When the *nez* spoke, her voice was raspy. 'Hmm, this is different. I...' she turned away as a commotion occurred outside the room.

Distracted, she swivelled back. 'I want to know more about what this scent means to you but a delivery of flowers has arrived.' The teacher turned to the class. 'Come, come, everyone and I will show you how the magic begins.'

Madam observed Kitty over her long, luscious lashes, before discarding the test strip and walking away. Kitty's shoulders slumped and she pressed her lips tight together. Clearly, the concoction wasn't *magnifique*. Oh well, that is why she'd enrolled in perfume school...to learn. Darn it, she closed the lid on the vial extra tight.

Following the other students, Kitty ambled out of the room. They were led down a narrow corridor and into a large factory room. Canvas bags were being unloaded from the tray of a truck reversed into the bay. Spilling over the top were bursts of bright purple flower petals. They appeared fragile to Kitty and worthy of being treated with care. Not so, those petals were being tossed with vigour onto trays. Kitty paused to smell, once again the scent was overwhelming. This time she was a child drinking Ribena, a blackcurrant fruit drink. Was it an Australian product? She didn't know but this flower aroma reminded her of the juice, only it was subtly different, yet still intoxicating. With no self-control, Kitty shoved her face into the canvas bag. Her fellow students laughed and Madame eyed her quizzically. She had no regrets, she wanted to tip those flowers up to her face and drown herself in their fragrance.

'This is *iris pallida*, native to Croatia but now grown here in Grasse. It's an elegant, special flower.' Kitty heard the teacher pause while another scent drifted into the room, overtaking the lavender.

'Ah, *bonjour, Monsieur Joubert.*' The name was familiar. Their teacher stood in front of the delivery men as they transferred the flowers onto trays. 'This is not your crop, no, you grow roses?' she asked him. He responded in French, but Kitty didn't catch it. Why do they speak so fast? It was impossible to understand.

As he spoke, his eyes lifted to take her in. The man was tall and wore a French beret with a long-sleeved shirt and shorts, simple closed in shoes on his feet. While he didn't look familiar, there was no mistaking the smell. It was him. That divine fragrance...Kitty swooned on the spot, her knees going weak while a flash of déjà vu hit. The bouquet was overwhelming and delicious and sucked all the air out of the factory. The man and his scent became the only person in the room. He moved closer and bowed his head. Kitty shifted her feet. What the hell was he doing? Then he shot a look sideways at the tiny vial in her hand and took it without asking, raised it to his nose, inhaled. Kitty saw the pulse in his neck beat as she waited for him to speak. Instead, he glanced sharply, with confidence, a jut of his chin, and those crystal-clear blue eyes pierced her.

Oh!

The teacher spoke and the moment was broken. He reached down to retrieve another hessian bag and got on with his job.

Kitty dragged her feet up the hill. At least she'd get fit during her stay in Grasse. Daily walks up this steep slope would do the trick.

As she approached the villa, the lights were blazing and the windows and doors open. A gentle breeze blew, so the accommodation would be cool. Luckily there weren't any mosquitoes like home.

Chatter and music drifted outdoors and Kitty paused at the main entrance. She desperately wanted to skulk around the back. Be damned if she wanted to see her experienced and qualified housemates. With one foot in the entrance, Madame Adrienne spied her, and it was too late to change her mind. Raph stood stirring at a large pot while his wife poured them a drink, and Kitty spotted the quick pat on his bottom before handing over the glass.

'Ah, *ma cherie*, lovely to have you home. Did you have a nice day?'

Sheesh, how did she answer that? Politely, like she'd been taught. 'Yes, thank you.'

'You are just in time for dinner. Please.' Adrienne gestured with her hand. 'Come in, I'll get you a drink.' She rushed around the kitchen, extracting another wine glass.

The kitchen smelled divine and Kitty's stomach grumbled. All she'd eaten today was her baguette and coffee. She might have to endure dinner with the others, but it seemed as if the food would be good.

'Here, my love, take this and head on through. There's bread on the table and everyone is here.' Adrienne offered her an encouraging smile, and with a nod of her head, she returned to the kitchen.

Best get it over with. Taking tiny steps and matching sips, Kitty entered the dining room.

'She's back!' Chad announced.

'Why weren't you on the tour this morning? You're going to be behind in classes next week.'

'You're late.'

'Where have you been all day?'

Questions were thrown at her from all directions but she thought it best to ignore them. Unfortunately, standing there like a stunned deer meant someone had spotted her vial.

'Hey, what's this?' Sofia, the Italian girl, snatched it out of Kitty's hands.

Argh, what an idiot! With the stress of arriving home, she'd forgotten to throw it away, hide it, anything.

'Can you please give that back? It's mine.'

That was resolutely ignored as Sofia opened the lid and smelled. She blanched. 'Oh, *mama mia*! What is this?'

'It's nothing.' Kitty tried to reclaim it but the small jar was passed around the table.

'Is this a perfume?' asked Marianna in her Spanish twang. 'Something went very wrong.'

By the time the little bottle reached Chad's mate, Pete, Kitty was done being polite. She ripped it out of his hands, shoved it into her bag and sat with a thump at the only spare seat. Ignoring the awkward silence, she picked up a bread roll, dipped it in the olive oil and ate, eyes downcast.

The English girl, Julia, broke the silence. 'You're not on the course, are you?' She stared Kitty down, waiting for a reply.

'No.'

Everyone shouted at once. 'Told you they wouldn't accept you without a degree.'

'It's a highly sought-after qualification, they don't just let anyone in.'

'Probably for the best.'

Adrienne and Raph entered with plates of steaming food and bowls of salad.

'Adrienne! Did you hear? Kitty isn't on the course. Can she even stay here, then? Isn't this place exclusively for the students of the Perfume Institute?'

Bloody Chad. Kitty turned in her seat and glowered at him. What the actual heck? Now she couldn't stay here either?

Adrienne had placed her dishes down and put her hand to Kitty's shoulder. 'Is that true, you aren't on the course? What will you do?'

'I am studying...only it's the other perfume course. The one run by *Beaumont de Villiers*.'

The room erupted in laughter, and Kitty's cheeks flushed.

Raph clapped his hands, and the din stopped. 'That's enough now. Everyone is welcome here. Anyone who wants to visit our beautiful city of Grasse and learn more about our ancient and beloved practice of perfume-making is welcome in my home.' He approached Kitty and stopped to cup her face before kissing her on both cheeks. He rose to stand next to Adrienne and wrapped one arm around her shoulders.

The couple stood behind her chair in solidarity. The students wisely turned their attention back to the food, and Kitty ate in silence.

Chapter Five

To Kitty, the faded bronze building appeared like an oasis in a world of uncertainty. Her chest filled with joy, and excitement bubbled within.

It was Monday, and she was finally commencing her studies. She was on the path to becoming a perfumer. These studies would secure her future, a future in which she didn't rely upon anyone else to fulfil her dreams.

Shading her eyes, she gazed at the building as if it held her destiny in its hands. Ah, she was getting ahead of herself, but it was hard not to want to reach out and grasp her dreams, hold on tight, and not let go. But perhaps she needed to start class first. It was hard not to be anxious. She'd been wandering the streets of Grasse killing time *for hours*.

The Institute of Perfumery class had commenced early this morning. Her course began after lunch. Kitty was itching to get started...why couldn't her class begin after breakfast, too?

But seriously, how could a school with such a wonderful

name not be fabulous? She whispered the words for the hundredth time. *Ecole du Beau Parfum*. The school was surely named for her.

Given that she was early, she was ushered into an empty room with desks and chairs. Not a lab? Her mind skipped back to the room at the Institute that housed the equipment you needed to make perfume. Kitty glanced around the bare space; she was sure there'd be other rooms.

Her phone pinged with the arrival of a text. Swiping left, Stuart's name popped up. Oh! Her heart jumped into her throat. It was the first time he'd contacted her since his last, brief message. Reading the short missive, she devoured each word. He was sorry; he hoped she was okay; is there anything he could do?

Yes! Turn back time and not break up with her! Too late for that, wasn't it? Why was he being so nice? It was so confusing. He no longer loved her after five years together but waited until she was ready to walk down the aisle on the happiest day of her life, before he chose to tell her. Had he ever loved her? They'd had a wonderful life together, or so she'd thought.

None of it made sense, and she couldn't reconcile his actions with the text. The only answer was another woman, but she'd been scouring through his social media pages and had found no evidence of that. Luckily, her classmates arrived, filled up the room with their chatter and Kitty put her phone away.

Their teacher followed, wearing a white laboratory coat. Finally, a good sign. They must be getting straight to work. Kitty extracted her notebook and pencil from her bag and sat up straight; a familiar aroma filled the space. She frowned trying to place the scent when she spied their teacher. The man from the office; the dashing Frenchman who reminded her of green tea.

It wasn't exactly a scent to make a girl swoon, but he was a Clarke Kent lookalike. Perfect, because she was sworn off men and could concentrate on what he taught instead. He spoke… talking about perfume was enough to keep her interest, but it didn't hurt that he was nice to look at, either. Each word sent a thrill racing up her spine. The combination of his sexy accent and handsome features had her mesmerised.

Her pen remained poised in the air, seemingly forgetting what it was meant to do.

'*Bonjour*, my name is Henri.' He pronounced it with elongated letters like *Henree*. 'I am the CEO of Beaumont de Villiers, the oldest perfume company in Grasse. I run this course to help others learn the ancient art of perfume-making. You will learn the secrets behind what we do. At de Villiers we do not open our factory to the public, nor run day classes or operate a museum; it is all about the perfume. So, this state-of-the-art course will provide you with a clear and comprehensive understanding of the fundamentals instrumental to making perfume. And you will learn about my company. We will cover perfumery and structure, classification and storytelling, in addition to understanding the consumer experience and the selling of fragrance. You will learn about each step of the process.'

Kitty's heart sped up. Finally, she was going to learn about perfume. Relief swept through her as she inched forward in her seat, eager to hear everything Henri said. At last, she was where she belonged.

His gaze landed on her as if he could read her mind and she inhaled sharply under his intense stare. Her breath hitched, but then he moved on to the next person.

Kitty repositioned her pen ready to take notes.

Five hours later her hand cramped but she refused to stop scribbling. Henri hadn't paused to take breath in their first class, nor stopped for a coffee or toilet break, but that suited her perfectly. Her first day was over in a blink. Her classmates packed up their belongings and Kitty sank back into the real world.

Her mind was filled with ideas: of perfume, scent and smell. Keen to remain in this world a moment longer, she lingered, slowly returning her notebook to her bag when a shadow fell over her. The waft of woody undergrowth tickled her nose.

Kitty looked up as Henri sat on the corner of the desk opposite hers. Earth and musk tones overwhelmed her. She closed her eyes and willed the scent of this gorgeous man to sweep her away to another place.

For once, it didn't.

Opening her eyes, Kitty stole a glance at him from under her lashes. Her breath caught; he was more attractive close up: chiselled jaw, smooth skin with no hint of a five o'clock shadow, an angular face with short, thick dark hair.

She willed her expression to cooperate and ordered her lips into a smile.

'Hello. Did you enjoy the class?' Dimples appeared in his cheeks when he finally spoke.

Oh, the cuteness. 'Yes, I did, thank you. It was wonderful.'

'Your accent. Are you from New Zealand or Australia?' A grin revealed straight, white teeth.

'I'm Australian.'

'Oh, Australian, how wonderful. You've travelled all this way to Grasse to learn from me?'

Kitty swallowed. 'Yes. I want to be a perfumer.'

He nodded. Dark broody eyes considered her. 'Would you like to have a drink with me? We can chat some more?'

Was she seriously being asked out by her teacher? Should her answer be hell, yes, or hell, no? And what about her commitment to learning?

A strange tussle commenced in the pit of her stomach rendering her breathless and lost for words, so she simply nodded and stood. He held her chair out and tucked it under the desk when she was clear, before he hurried to open the door.

Outside, the day had disappeared into dusk and the heat had fizzled away to the cooler air of early evening. Unlike at home, the light here in the Cote D'Azur wouldn't fade for hours yet.

As they walked side by side through the bustling alleyways, Henri moved closer until their shoulders were touching.

'What is this scent?' he asked, leaning in towards her before retreating.

'My perfume? This is one I picked up here in Grasse the other day. It was on sale at the chemist. It reminded me of home.'

He nodded but didn't make further comment.

'It's the first time I've worn a different scent. I've always worn Montgomery Perfumes. They are Australian. I used to work there.'

'Ah, so you have some experience of perfume?'

'Yes.' She grinned. Soon he would discover she wasn't like the other students in her class. They didn't know the basics she understood.

When they reached the bar, Henri ushered her inside a narrow and low door. Luckily, she didn't want to admire the view, as Henri had taken her to a trendy bar down a set of long stairs to a basement. The grey lounge chairs were decorated with mustard yellow and burnt orange cushions. Black-and-white prints hung on slate walls. People lounged around, talking with their hands and enjoying their drinks.

Henri ordered their drinks and they sat in facing plush armchairs. Kitty twisted her fingers together in her lap. She hadn't dated anyone but Stuart, except a few disastrous dates before him, and they'd met when she was nineteen. To say she was out of practice was an understatement. But this wasn't a date, was it? A drink with a friend? Colleague? Her mind was racing when she found some words to break the silence.

'So, you are the oldest perfume company in Grasse?'

He sipped champagne, and she hid her surprise that was his drink of choice. A man drinking sparkling? A nice change from the Aussie blokes at home enjoying their stubbies of beer.

She sipped hers and relished the crisp bubbles. Kitty placed the glass to her nose to inhale the fizz. 'So fruity, such fresh char-acter,' she muttered out loud.

He tilted his head and stared at her then. His dark eyes pene-trated deep down inside her, igniting a sizzle she'd never felt so strongly before.

'I think you know a lot about smell, yes?'

Wow, he'd be the only person in Grasse to say so. But after days of knockbacks and feeling ridiculously stupid, Kitty soaked up the praise.

'Yes, Montgomery was small, family-owned like your company. There is something about working with family and striving towards similar goals. I was hoping to progress within the ranks and work with their perfumer, who is French, by the way...' Her words died away then. It was too early to reveal her story to a stranger. Even though she'd hoped that one day, she and Stuart would be running the perfume company together. Taking another sip, she swallowed those words back down, and, with them, her lost dreams.

'You may be too good for our course.' Henri touched her hand and shivers raced up her spine. The tips of his fingers were cold from the chilled glass. 'I think we have a lot in common.'

Do we? Despite the touch of this good-looking man, it felt a bit like a business meeting. She crossed her legs, and his eyes skittered to the bare skin revealed by her denim shorts.

'When will we make perfume?'

His smile was tight yet whimsical. He glanced away before replying. 'We have some more to learn before then.'

That's all she wanted to know.

'I will arrange a private tour of Beaumont de Villiers for you. Later in the week we have an excursion to another manufacturer in Grasse which is our fiercest competitor. They operate less traditionally and offer tours, classes etcetera. They are open to the public and make soap!' He exaggerated the last word and shivered before finishing his drink in one gulp and placing it on the low table between them.

'Now, I must run.' Leaning in, he kissed her slowly, languorously on each cheek. Kitty felt the indelible outline of his full, luscious lips on her skin. By the time she opened her eyes, he was gone.

Chapter Six

'It is almost ready, *oui*?' Mrs Roubillard offered Pierre Joubert a steaming cup of morning café as he stood in the flower field. 'I don't have your nose, but even I can smell the difference. Harvest is upon us.'

To reach this point, it had been a year of endless pruning and nurturing the tiny pink buds. The blossoming rows of flowers filled him with the most beautiful longing and happiness, and simultaneously dread, guilt, and despair. Harvest was both his favourite time of year and his most loathed. And that is exactly why his housekeeper and best friend, Mrs Roubillard, was kind to him, regardless of his behaviour.

Pierre accepted the coffee and sipped as he gazed at his precious rose centifolia spread in the acres before him. The world tilted back to rights and the scratchiness in his eyes reduced with the comfort of the hot drink. Thank goodness for Mrs Roubillard, she returned normalcy to the day, reminding him it was morning. He hadn't yet slept.

'*Oui,* next week we harvest,' Pierre answered. He had been out in the field since the first dawn light cracked over the horizon. Returning home from his night out where he'd drunk way too much and flirted with too many women, the flower fields had been the perfect place to suffer through his hangover. And work through other issues, or more so, forget about them.

Being amongst his flowers always soothed him. His mind might be a mess and his body depleted of rest and hydration, but he smiled broadly at Mrs Roubillard. If only he could stay out here all day.

'Are you okay?'

He nodded, afraid to speak lest his voice might give way.

'We will have the children here again?' she pressed.

That thought brought a ray of sunshine. 'Yes, definitely. I must arrange their visit.'

'It's one of my favourite days of the year.'

'Mine, too,' he replied, but he knew what she was doing. The woman was smart. Making him think of happier times, but it would never work. It didn't matter what he did or thought, it would never change the past. Mrs Roubillard shifted her feet, anxious for him to prepare for work. It never ceased to puzzle him why she worried about him so much. But in a world devoid of hope and happiness, it caused a tender ache to flash across his chest.

To avoid her scrutiny, he nuzzled Buster, his Boxer dog. His companion leaned against his leg while he rubbed his ears and neck. The dog hadn't had much sleep either, keeping guard next to him while he tended his garden. But not too close, Buster knew the rules; he was not allowed in the flower rows. There must never be any risk to the crop.

'Where's your pal?' Buster had a dog friend, Theo, who wasn't half as keen on losing sleep. 'I've got to get to work, so you better go and find him.' With one last pat to his butt, the dog wandered off obediently.

Mrs Roubillard waited and reality beckoned. There was no chance she'd leave him alone any longer. The clock ticked on the start of another work day while the weight of his thoughts bore down on him. He willed the flowers to work their magic. Useless beliefs, even though being out here had helped even if his chest remained heavy like a stone was lodged there. Pierre hardly noticed the pain anymore, it lived within him, a permanent ache, a reminder. As if he'd ever forget. No matter what he did the month of May brought with it not only harvest, but painful memories of mistakes in the past.

It was best not to be alone with his dark thoughts. They led to nothing but heartache. Too much time spent thinking led to dwelling on what he could not change.

'I have pastries in the courtyard and more fresh coffee.' She raised her eyebrows at him, indulging him once more. The woman was a saint who ignored him returning home drunk at disgraceful hours of the morning and often in terrible circumstances after a bust-up or two. After all, he had a reputation to uphold. It was easy to misbehave and get away with it when that was expected of you. But he drew the line at bringing women back here, to his home; he'd never show Mrs Roubillard that side of him. He knew she wouldn't judge; she only cared for him. None of it mattered anyway, as long as he kept turning up at the factory each day and making brilliant perfume, he'd be left alone.

'Will you join me?' he asked as he sat at the outdoor furniture. She frowned in response, poured his second coffee, placed a pastry on his plate and swung a feather duster to and fro. 'I've got work to do.' The light touch of her hand on his shoulder before she departed caused a sob to catch in his throat. How could she love him?

His phone rang with an unidentified number that he ignored. Moments later, it dinged with the arrival of a message. The hot coffee scorched his throat as he listened to a voicemail from a woman. Someone from last night, apparently. Someone who remembered him well. Memories flitted in the back of his mind but didn't gain any traction. Pierre swiped delete.

Unable to resist, he stood and strode across to the nearest bush, bent low until his face was amongst the petals and breathed in. The scent surged through him as if it was air offering life. It enlivened him. He was excited for the blooms to open but also for their increased aroma that would fill his entire patch with his favourite smell. Low to the ground, he collected a handful of dirt and let it run through his fingers. It was dark and dense and rich. His connection to the land that fed, housed and enriched his flowers was primal. The urge to protect and nurture his crop was overwhelming. He would lay down and die for these flowers and his farm.

Footsteps thudded down the low set of stairs from the house. He turned to meet Mrs Roubillard. She blew out her cheeks and rushed across to him, her apron strings blowing out behind her.

He might love his flowers the most, but she came a close second.

'Okay, okay.' Pierre held his hand up and laughed. 'I'm going.'

'You'll be late,' she said.

Yes. And remember, my parents return today, so I'll be dining with them tonight.' He hated the look of pity she sent in his direction. Anything but pity: anger, disappointment, bad luck, regret would be better. 'It'll be fine. They've had a long trip overseas and will be in a good mood and have lots of stories, no doubt.'

Mrs Roubillard nodded, acknowledging that she wouldn't say any more.

'Maybe tonight you can come directly home. I'll make you a nightcap.' It was a direction coated in hope. He couldn't bear to look at her and make promises he knew he wouldn't keep. Didn't want to think about the disappointment he might cause. But maybe tonight he would. Perhaps it was time to break the cycle.

'Have a good day,' and he kissed her on the forehead in farewell.

Kitty fingered the edge of her battered notebook. Only two days into the course the pages overflowed with her lessons on the history of perfume, its origins in Grasse and the foundation of Beaumont de Villiers. Like a plant starved of rainfall, she'd listened, taken copious notes and recited them back later. Before falling asleep at night, she quizzed herself on what she'd learned. An earthquake might hit Grasse, and she'd never know, such was her engagement with finally learning about perfume.

She had loved learning about the mechanics of perfume, but it was day three and time to get to the nuts and bolts of perfume-making, the 101 practical guide if you like. Kitty had waited her whole life for this.

Henri entered the classroom and glanced immediately in her direction, where she sat in the centre of the front row. His gaze lingered, heat simmered in his eyes and he offered a tight smile, with a slight nod of his head.

His gesture was like a physical touch, a stroking of a dying fire, ratcheting her body temperature from mild to hot. Did the other students notice the special attention? Kitty glanced around but the group was busy chatting amongst themselves or scrolling through their phones, waiting for the class to begin.

The French were so charismatic. How did they learn this skill? Genes or culture? Who knew? But as quickly as she'd soaked in his attention, the sensation wore off. What was she doing wallowing in the look of her French perfume teacher? Was she that shallow? That starved of affection? Well, yes, probably.

Henri interrupted these thoughts. 'Today we have a special surprise. We are touring one of the only other large perfume-making factories and dynasties of Grasse, after Beaumont, of course, and that is the *House of Joubert*.'

Exclamations of excitement erupted around the classroom but Kitty's whole body lit up from the inside as waves of happiness rolled through her. Her wish had come true! Time to learn the real art.

Henri shushed them as he said they'd first learn about the top, middle and base notes and the structure of fragrance before the tour. Kitty pulled out her pen and wrote down every word.

An hour later Kitty bounced on her toes as she waited in line to enter the pink palace once more. She was eager to return and do better this time. Practice until her fragrance was perfect. She couldn't wait to get started.

With her fellow classmates, she entered the private back area of the *House of Joubert*, only open to those on tour. Anyone could tour, of course; she and her classmates were not special in that regard, but still, she felt out of the ordinary. Their glamorous tour guide, with her dark hair rolled into an elegant bun, kept Kitty captivated. Perhaps she simply loved everything French?

'Creating a perfect perfume is to tell a story. It is most often linked to a personal life experience. And therefore, each experience will be individual. Because what the perfume says about you will be different to any other consumer.'

This was a point of difference between *House of Joubert* and *Beaumont de Villiers*. Joubert told a love story as they spoke of perfume, of its creation, of its personal elements. Henri talked about perfume as a formula, a chemical concoction and the best had the right elements. She thought both were correct but she soaked up the quixotic version.

Their guide continued. 'The story that you conceptualise makes its way onto paper. You add raw materials which form the soul and skeleton of the perfume and to that, you include sometimes dozens of other essences, a bit like composing a piece of music or a poem.'

Maybe that's where she was going wrong, Kitty had no idea how to write poetry.

As their guide detailed the machinations of perfume, the group entered the shed that Kitty had already seen.

'This is where the raw ingredients of flowers are placed onto trays over vats of water that boil and the process is called extraction. As the steam rises, it captures the scent-bearing components of the flower and carries it into a glass cooler where the mixture of water and essential oils are collected.' The guide gestured to the large, steel vats. She learned it was the maceration or filtering room where the perfume concentrate was mixed with alcohol and left for several weeks. Finally, the alcohol is separated from the fragrant substance to obtain the absolute, which is the concentrated liquid used in perfume.

Kitty itched to write this down but instead placed it into her memory. It was easy, really. There was harvesting, extraction, distillation and then expression. She recited these words over and over as they walked into a room of production lines. Her heart sank, but making perfume and commercial perfume on a large scale was a business. But Kitty knew that before there was a production line with conveyor belts, one of the infamous noses of the house would have created the perfume that was then mass-produced. Another room had glass beakers, tubes, vials and bronze vats. No perfumers worked today. This liquid was bottled into those gorgeous pink glass jars with gold lids.

The voices receded as Kitty found herself drawn to a private enclave with a small bench and various vials. She lifted the first. After extracting the lid, she closed her eyes to capture the very essence of the scent. It was undeniably musk. And divine. Musk was an important ingredient, particularly for men's cologne. Then there was lavender, another scent of her grandmother, perhaps of grandmothers everywhere.

'What are you doing in here?'

Shit.

Kitty turned, vial still in hand and there *he* was. The exotic-smelling Frenchman from the train station on her very first day. Even amongst the varied and abundant scents surrounding them in the lab, his aroma, he, stood out.

His scent was different today. The undertone of rose was overwhelming, like he'd bathed in it. There was not a more renowned and popular feminine scent than rose. Subtle, distinct, beautiful, but not usually worn by a man. Kitty swayed with the aroma and wanted to swim in it too, perhaps with him…

'Um, I'm on the tour with the *Ecole du Beau Parfum*.'

He ignored her reply. 'What perfume are you wearing?' His head titled in a seductive manner, like he was going to sweep his lips along her collarbone up to her jawline. *Gulp.* Did he always do that? Kitty almost bowed to the moment, wanting to wrap around him and snuggle in, to feel the press of his lips against her creamy pale skin. Would his kiss feel different to Stuart? He was so close his warm breath brushed against her skin.

Then he titled his head in a brusque manner, like he was irritated and his nose twitched. He waited on her response.

'Oh, it's called *White Flowers*. I bought it here, at the chemist.' She was about to ask him if he liked it, but something in the twist of his expression stopped her. He remained standing close to her invading her personal space and she didn't mind one bit.

'White Flowers,' he scoffed. 'That is a very unoriginal name assuming it is made of white flowers. What is the flower? Jasmine? Iris?'

Kitty somehow thought he knew exactly what the flower was, but she'd play along. 'Magnolia.' She didn't say she'd bought it because it reminded her of home. Here, right in this moment, she realised it had been a stupid idea.

'Hmm.' He leaned in again, not so close this time. 'Yes, and the other ingredients?'

She rattled them off. 'I was told it was one of their top sellers. That it's very popular.'

'Is it?' The words dripped with sarcasm. His eyes diverted to the vial still in her hand. Quickly, she remembered where she was and replaced it. 'What is that one?' he asked.

'Hyacinth'

He held up the last in the row. Kitty leaned in and knew the answer immediately.

'Jasmine.'

He chose another.

'Hmm, peppermint.' She loved that smell.

It was an interrogation she was passing with flying colours. She assumed she'd answered correctly because he neither confirmed nor denied her response to each. It was the serious squint in his crystal-clear ocean eyes and the clenched jaw that had her assuming he was impressed.

Someone approached from behind them. 'Mr Joubert, I'm so sorry. We lost one of the students,' her guide gushed.

Dawning realisation hit Kitty. He was *the* Joubert, the *House of Joubert* itself. Kitty had been so engrossed in the very essence of his smell that she hadn't realised he wasn't dressed like a delivery man or a factory worker today. He cut a fine figure in a dark as midnight suit, outrageously gorgeous baby pink tie with the slightest reveal of the same colour socks. His hair was perfectly coiffured and slicked into place, excepting a few tight curls that escaped and framed his face. A sizeable diamond stud sparkled in his left earlobe.

'Come on.' The guide ushered her along. 'We must finish the tour. Everyone is waiting.'

She and Mr Joubert exchanged a heated look before he offered a curt nod.

Kitty caught up with the group in the shop. Damn her budget. She searched the shelves for the cheapest fragrance. A tiny delicate bottle of eau de toilette was all she could afford, and the price was eye-watering. She never wore the watered-down version that contained only between five and fifteen percent of the perfume essence. If you were going to wear a scent, it had to be concentrate or eau de parfum; why else bother? Eau de parfum had between ten and twenty percent essence and was stronger.

At the counter, Kitty refused to think about the sum of money she was handing over for the bottle. She distracted herself with the available trinkets and spotted a flyer.

Tour a real-life flower farm, come to where it all begins. Kitty tucked that into her bag.

Chapter Seven

'Bonjour, mademoiselle, *puis-je vous aider*?'

Kitty let the words wash over her. The glamour of the language was universal, and Kitty hoped she would never become immune.

Her blank stare must have given away her confusion and the woman repeated the question in English.

Kitty held up the flyer. 'I'm here for a tour.'

The woman's brow furrowed, and she looked over her shoulder. 'Ah, *oui*, of course.'

Kitty double-checked the address to ensure she was in the right place. *Yep.* At the rumble of an engine, she glanced back up to watch a bus park in the bay outside the elaborate metal gate entrance. As soon as the doors whooshed open, a group of Asian tourists were ushered past her into the farm entrance.

Kitty still clutched the handlebars of the bicycle she'd borrowed from the villa. Searching around for a safe spot, she leaned it against the back of the gate.

'*Bonjour, mesdames et messieurs. Bienvenue et suivez-moi s'il vous plait.*' The woman gestured for them to follow her.

Ah, the bouquet of fragrances. Kitty spotted the fields of flowering blooms immediately, but it was the scent that hit her first. The rose centifolia. The May rose it was sometimes called. It was one of the most special raw ingredients for perfume and was only harvested a couple of weeks per year. Kitty understood some of the most prestigious perfume houses either owned or contracted to flower farms in the Grasse region and had exclusive rights over the crop. Imagine being a flower farmer for Chanel? She wondered whether this farm contracted directly to the *House of Joubert*. She couldn't wait to find out.

The group wandered down the long drive. Farming must pay because they passed an incredible house; it appeared more like a French chateau or castle. Made of stone common in the region, it was grand and wide with the most gorgeous viewing section at the top of three- stories. Below was a sweeping balcony and the windows had white-washed shutters that were also popular in the area. In front of the house was a pond that matched the width of the house, where ducks glided effortlessly. In the middle was a cherub water fountain shooting water into the air. Mildew and moss covered the surface of the baby's round bottom. A garden of hardy plants and bushes surrounded the ledge and outdoor dining area. The light stone of the house contrasted with the green hues of the trees, with the burst of colour coming from the surrounding flower fields.

Kitty clutched her hands to her chest at the sight. What a divine place to drink a cocktail and watch the sunset after a day in the fields. Caught up in her daydreams she had to stride to catch the group that had moved ahead of her.

Their guide introduced herself as Mrs Roubillard. She spoke tentatively and kept glancing over her shoulder, as if expecting or wanting someone to arrive any minute and save her from the tour.

Except for tourists snapping photos and talking in their language, the area was quiet. There weren't any farmers or other staff. It was only the flowers and their beauty. Kitty was enthralled.

Their guide informed them that the farm harvested exclusively to the *House of Joubert* but was one of many contractors they engaged to produce the flowers they needed for the perfumes. Tonnes of flower buds produced the tiniest amount of concentrate. Members of the group posed next to the flower bushes, taking selfies. Kitty didn't want photographs of herself, she wanted the remember each fold of the petal and their delicious aroma.

Imagine working all year to produce a crop that was harvested in a matter of days to only produce perfume essence? It was mind boggling to her that these gorgeous flowers in front of her would become beautiful perfumes.

'Come, *mademoiselle*, follow me, we'll head to the packing rooms.' Kitty was distracted with her head bowed to the middle of a bush. She got the gist, though, and followed the group.

Off to the side of the impressive house stood a row of sheds housing tractors and equipment. One larger open room held the hessian bags used to hold the flowers when picking. Mrs Roubillard collected a white cloth apron and showed them how to wear it. Then she imitated the motion of picking: pluck, pluck, pluck. Then she demonstrated the act of throwing the filled bags onto trucks for transportation.

'We pick next week,' she said. 'Always early.'

Members of the group took the opportunity to snap more pictures next to the tractor, the empty bench and the grand barn-style door. Kitty wandered into another room, off to the right. Inside was cooler and long benches at each edge and a large window overlooked the verdant green hills.

A lab! How strange, she thought. It mirrored the labs she'd seen at the perfume factory, simply with less equipment and on a smaller scale.

'It seems you like disappearing into places you are not permitted to go.'

That voice. Husky, deep and like music feeding her soul. Kitty turned.

Oh, la.

'You look terrible.' The words blurted out before she could stop them.

Mr Joubert released a joyous chuckle, like he hadn't laughed for a while. But she spoke the truth. The man in front of her looked nothing like the immaculate man of yesterday. Today, his curls sat out of control and unruly around his face. A heavy shadow of stubble lined his chin, and his eyes were bloodshot.

Still damn hot, though.

'Is this your farm?'

He leaned forward. Kitty sucked in a quick breath, but he proceeded to kiss her on both cheeks. 'My name is Pierre Joubert. This is my flower farm and where I live; it is my home amongst the pink petals.'

'I love pink.' She couldn't help herself, and regretted her words straight away.

Instead of laughing again, the corners of his eyes crinkled as he smiled. 'So do I.'

He paused, and she realised he was waiting for her introduction.

'I'm Katherine Landry, but everyone calls me Kitty.' He watched her lips before moving his gaze upwards to her eyes. That smouldering gaze set off a bonfire burning in the pit of her stomach.

'That's a beautiful name.' The timbre of his voice dropped an octave. 'Can I assume you are interested in the art of perfume making?'

'Yes, yes. I'm here in Grasse to become a perfumer.' He gazed at her again, the edges of his eyes still crinkled. His mind seemed to tick over as he watched her. She released a breath when he didn't laugh.

'It is a tradition, a skill that is learned over many years. You must have an incredible sense of smell; some people simply don't have it. If you are lucky enough to have it, then it takes time to cultivate the skill and learn how to make beautiful perfume.' He pronounced "beautiful" with exaggerated intonation and Kitty's knees trembled.

'I'm trying to learn as much as I can,' she said without looking at him.

'At the Institute?'

Damn it! She shook her head but didn't elaborate. He waited. *'Ecole du Beau Parfum.'*

A flicker of something swept across his features but was too fast for her to capture. 'Of course, that is why you were at the factory yesterday. On the tour. Beaumont de Villiers do not provide tours, only us.' If he was trying to make a point, she didn't understand it.

'I was impressed yesterday with your recognition of essences. Was that luck?'

She shook her head and her loose, wavy blonde hair slipped across her face.

'Where did you learn it?' Pierre tilted his handsome face to the side.

'Um, I worked at a perfume house in Australia...I picked up a few things there...'

'Picked up? In a lab working with creators?' he interrupted.

'No, I worked in the shop.' She rushed on, 'but I've always had the ability to distinguish scents and remember them.'

'Your family are in perfume?'

'No.'

He shook his head. 'I can't believe your ability to detect scent if you didn't grow up in that environment. Incredible.' His last word was a whisper, as if he didn't quite believe it. 'I learned from my father who learned from his and so on.'

Kitty sighed. 'I would have loved that, but there was no one to teach me. While I can recognise the scents, I can't seem to put them together and make a beautiful perfume.'

'How many times have you tried?'

'Once.'

'*Non, non.* It takes much practice. Come, let me show you.' Pierre took her hand and guided her to a table with equipment she was becoming very familiar with. He tugged her close, their bodies almost touching. Out of the corner of her eye, Kitty saw Mrs Roubillard approach, pause, and leave again without interrupting.

'What story should we tell today? What will go into our perfume?' he mused.

Kitty wracked her brain for elements.

'Jasmine?'

He turned sharply and their arms brushed. A strange tingling rippled beneath her skin at the exact spot of their contact.

'*Non*. Not ingredients. What is our story to tell? What imagery do we want our wearer to conjure when they place it to the nape of their neck?' His fingers reached across and touched just below her right ear. Her skin warmed as if she'd been brushed by a flame.

Kitty swallowed and said, 'Love.' The romantic in her blurted that out without thinking. She wished she would pause before speaking.

He smiled, tight-lipped, almost a smirk, but didn't argue. 'Tell me about love? Is it sweet? Hot? Spicy?' His words lingered on her skin like a caress.

'It is pretty and pink. A warm glow that intensifies.'

Pierre kept his head bowed but nodded and gathered in front of him several glass vials. He opened the tight cap on one and inhaled as he held it to his nose. This went on for too long and Kitty grew impatient to know more. It was like he was drawing that very essence into the deep, dark recess of his soul.

'This is what you describe. This is my rose, from the farm. The rose centifolia. To look at it is soft, pretty and pink but it has depth and substance and you can rely upon it.' Instead of passing the vial to her, he held it up to her nose. She took a short, sharp whiff. He shook his head again. 'No, deep inhale, really smell it.' Kitty closed her eyes and let the scent envelop her. It was everything he described.

With deliberate words and actions, he took her through each layer and demonstrated why he chose to add that note. It was incredible that he could improve upon the raw essence that already seemed perfect to her. But he did improve it, demonstrating he was a master perfumer at work.

He produced the finished creation it what seemed like minutes but was surely longer. It was only ten millilitres in a transparent glass bottle, and there were no fancy trims like at the factory. He rummaged around on the desk and located a small white sticky label and texta.

'This is your perfume. We shall call it *Kitty L'Amour.*' His words purred in Kitty's ears. He captured a drop of scent to his fingers and placed it once, twice, to the spot below both ears. The effect was instant as though it put her under a spell. It was a divine scent and he'd made it for her. They stood together like that for a moment, both savouring the smell and the experience. Pierre gazed at the vial.

Oh, to be gazed at like that.

But Kitty had other ideas. 'Pierre...Mr Joubert?'

'*Oui.*'

'Can I come and help you harvest next week?'

'*Oui.*'

<h1 style="text-align:center">Chapter Eight</h1>

Kitty was late. She skidded into her afternoon class, sliding across the linoleum floor on the soles of her ballet flats. The door didn't latch and slammed against the wall before she slumped into a seat at the back of the room. Heads turned in her direction while Henri paused mid-sentence and flicked her a dismissive glance.

Kitty caught her breath and reached for her belongings. The time had gotten away from her on her farm visit. She was still hot and sweaty from her encounter with Pierre. Or was it the fast cycle down the main street? She was pretty sure it was the former.

Back in the moment, she tried to concentrate on Henri. Yet, today, his monotone voice made the words blend into each other, and it became hard to focus. There'd be little chance of learning much today.

Henri talked of storytelling and the classification of a fragrance. That caught her attention as the contrast to how

Pierre described it was significant. Henri spoke of chemicals and components and what a consumer expected. Some, he said, wanted to be transported to an exotic location; others wanted to surround themselves in floral beauty; men, perhaps, wanted to appear brute and rugged, lathered in tough, outdoor smells.

Kitty agreed with what he said, but she couldn't help but remember how Pierre spoke with such emotion and passion about the creation of fragrance. Was it like cooking, she wondered? Her grandmother had sworn by baking with love, and that made the food taste better. Was perfume the same?

Henri asked the class the same question. What did they want a perfume to evoke? A sense of time, place or an experience? A lady at the front piped up and said flowers.

Well, damn. Kitty understood now. Perfume came from flowers; they were the very essence of it, but the final scent should not be floral. In fact, she thought that was all rather boring. Wouldn't it be unique and different to have a scent smell like something else?

Kitty knew what she would produce when she had the skills. As usual, she worried her ideas were outlandish.

A shadow crept across her desk. The hours had passed and Henri stood over her. 'Have dinner with me?' He lifted her hand for his traditional greeting. He'd forgiven her for being late.

She offered him a languorous smile. 'I'd love to,' she replied. Anything to get out of returning to the guest house and keeping company with her studious housemates who talked relentlessly about chemical particles that she didn't understand. She'd never felt so stupid.

It was too early for dinner after class, though. The French never ate before eight o'clock at the earliest and usually at nine.

So, she assumed they might enjoy an aperitif and nibblies. She was wrong.

Outside, Henri grasped her petite hand in his rough and thick fingers before urging her along. He walked a step ahead, and she followed his lead. They proceeded around the back of the school building and he opened the passenger door to dark blue, sedan Volvo car.

'Oh, where are we going?'

Henri ensured she was safely secured in the passenger seat before closing the door. He raced around to his side and jumped in before replying. 'I thought I'd take you somewhere special, a place with a view of the incredible Mediterranean Sea. You can't travel to the French Riviera and only see the quaint streets of Grasse. We are close to some of the most beautiful coastal areas of France. I'm taking you to Antibes.'

'Antibes! Oh, Henri, thank you, how exciting!'

Henri grinned at her enthusiasm. 'Antibes is a resort town too, like the more famous Cannes and Nice, but it's smaller. There's this section of coast that hooks around, a bit like the coast of Italy, and juts right out onto the sea. At the most southern tip, there's a restaurant that feels like it's supported by the ocean.' His smile widened.

Instinctively, she reached over and touched his knee. It was toned and firm to touch. Henri dressed in his sensible suits with never a hair out of place. With his thick glasses, he always appeared serious, but underneath, it seemed he hid a body of steel. Kitty caressed the spot.

Henri kept his gaze on the road.

'Thank you. Thank you for taking me there. I haven't been

outside of Grasse yet.' She noticed the happy twinkle in his eye as he cracked a grin.

'You are welcome. I enjoy your company.'

Kitty enjoyed his. Henri reminded her of Stuart despite trying not to think of her ex. Reliable, responsible, good-looking. Important qualities in a partner. Plus, being with him was easy, they chatted amiably during the short thirty-minute drive and avoided any awkward silences.

Arriving in the old town, Henri parked next to a fort-wall made of the traditional sandstone where adjacent buildings with chimneys and antennae on their apex met the skyline. Below, waves crashed against the wall, sea spray splashing upwards.

'The view from the restaurant is even better.' He inched across the console and placed his arm around her shoulders, pulling her towards him in the tight confines of the car.

She snuggled in. 'Is that even possible? It's beautiful.'

Henri flicked a switch, and his window wound down, letting in the taste of salt and the sounds of the waves crashing. Nearby, cars zoomed past.

'Have you always wanted to make perfume?' she asked.

'*Oui*, of course. Perfume has been in our family for generations. There was nothing else I ever wanted to do. Plus, it was expected of me. There are many more perfume houses now, but we do well. We are financially secure, employ many hundreds of people and sell fragrances around the world. I think we have a lot in common.'

'Do you?' Other than perfume, Kitty couldn't think what that was.

'Yes, we both love beautiful perfume.'

True.

'You are a beautiful woman and come from an exotic country far away. You work hard, are reliable and diligent and not too crazy, I think. Not do adventurous things.'

Huh?

'Like what?' she asked before her mind got away from her.

'Um, say mountain biking?'

'You don't like cycling?' Had he seen her ride the bike?

'Not really. Or any activities where you get all, as you say, dirty.'

'What do you like to do when you aren't working?'

He smiled like the thought created happy memories for him. 'Always family. Spending time with them is special, but I like fish.'

'As in fishing?' Kitty couldn't imagine it.

He shook his head, 'No, fish in a tank with oxygen and little decorations.'

'Do you like cats?'

'No! They kill things with their mouths and bring them into the house.' He shuddered for effect.

She loved cats but didn't say so.

'What is your favourite perfume?' That seemed like safe territory.

He thought for a moment, gazing into her eyes and tracing a solitary finger down the side of her face and jawline. '*La Rose*,' he said.

'What are the ingredients?'

This time, he did laugh. 'Rose, of course.'

'If I have learned anything these last few days, it's that a fragrance is more than its flower origins. What are the other ingredients?'

'There's a hint of jasmine, saffron, some bergamot and mint, I think.'

'Floral perfumes are very popular. Don't you think it would be wonderful to create something different? Like, I don't know, a scent of the ocean or the beach or your favourite chocolate?' She giggled, feeling self-conscious.

'*Absolument pas*! You do not mess with what is perfect. *Beaumont de Villiers* prides itself on tradition and its signature scents. We have created the same scents for centuries and will do so for many more years to come.'

Kitty deflated a little. Did she have this perfume thing all wrong?

Henri turned in his seat so they faced one another. His right hand cupped her cheek while his other arm cradled her close. His warm breath brushed against her face, and ripples of goosebumps erupted on her skin. His fingers ran through the tangled hair surrounding her face before tucking it behind her ear. Those same fingers caressed along her chin, around her lips and across her eyes and forehead. It was gentle and soothing. Her lids fluttered closed. A gentle breeze swept through the car, and she wound her arms inside his jacket and around his back. His thigh brushed hers as she shifted.

Then he kissed her. His soft and warm lips sent the pit of her stomach into a wild swirl. The kiss was slow, deliberate and... restrained. Was Henri holding himself back? She wanted more.

Kitty kissed the pulsing hollow at the base of his neck before trailing kisses up towards his throat. He shifted back in his seat, but she found his earlobe and nibbled. Hunger built. Here in this place with its beauty and strangeness, wild abandon filled her.

As her lips caressed his skin, a collage of images emerged of two different men, one French and one Australian.

Those thoughts faded as Henri retreated, just as she wanted to kiss him more passionately, and knock those confusing images out of her head.

He sat back now, out of her reach. His rejection hurt, but she tried to brush it away. He placed a chaste kiss on her forehead and tucked her head into his chest. It felt like a father embracing his daughter, not the sentiment she wanted. Her forehead leaned against his torso as wave after wave of emotion hit her.

Desire. Hunger, followed by disappointment. Out of the blue, another thought hit her; Pierre wouldn't stop. He'd kiss her hard and passionately and in sensitive places that would make her squirm. Embarrassment heated her face, and Kitty pulled away. It should have been a very romantic moment, but instead, he offered her a boyish, innocent smile devoid of the passion she'd been hoping for.

'Let's eat. The restaurant is expecting us.' He moved to open the car door. 'Perhaps later, if we have time, I can show you my aquarium.' On the short walk to the restaurant, he recited the seventeen different varieties of fish he kept.

Kitty threw back the cotton sheet. Ever since sneaking back late into the villa, she'd been unable to sleep.

The open bay windows provided a divine cool breeze circulating around the room and gave her a view of a starry night and silvery crescent moon.

Romantic. Argh!

Getting out of bed, she moved closer to the window and held her palm against the glass. She couldn't stop thinking about Pierre and Henri. Touching her lips with her fingertips, she recalled the kiss with Henri and felt her body stir.

Damn. She should be thinking about perfume, not two incredibly handsome Frenchmen. But hell, after what she'd been through, she deserved to have some fun, didn't she? The trouble was it didn't feel like fun. Kitty Landers could date every man in Grasse if she wanted to. Not that she did, in fact, that was the last thing she wanted. Any sort of emotional connection would just complicate things.

Stay focused on the perfume, Kitty.

Her relationship with Stuart had never been difficult. He was a kind, gentle man who treated her well, was interested and interesting and had a fabulous family who had loved and welcomed her.

The French had a much different view of love; feisty, hot and something to be revered.

Passionate.

The kiss with Henri had been reserved but her hunger had surprised her. Reliving it in the hours since she'd realised that she and Stuart had not shared a passionate toe-curling kiss in a long time. That was normal, right? They'd been together for more than five years. The statistics said the honeymoon period wore off quickly, the sparks disintegrating, burning low.

Besides her heart now shattered into a million pieces, she felt stupid about the breakdown of their relationship. Something she hadn't processed since she'd left the country in a hurry after her humiliation.

But how had she not felt a shift in their relationship? It was true the wedding planning consumed them in the months beforehand, but again, as a couple in love, what was better than preparing for the happiest day of your life?

Research said men who cheated were master manipulators. So, if Stuart was with someone else, it seemed he had an amazing ability to keep cool and pretend like nothing was different. Honestly, Kitty found that hard to believe. Surely there was no one else? But over these past few hours, she came to a realisation that their passion had died, and she hadn't noticed.

Damn it, she loathed the idea that her mother might be right. She'd fought against the notion that true love didn't exist her entire adult life. Determined not to be like her parents, determined to prove them wrong. To prove that achieving a happy ever after was possible. Except...what if it wasn't? What if long-term unconditional, passionate love wasn't possible, and we could only enjoy fleeting moments of happiness that had you self-assured, confident, loved-up until, bam, something shifted, and you were alone once more? Only to start all over again with someone new.

Thirteen years after her parents had divorced her mother still hated her father with real, and raw bitterness. Still carried around the wound of her failed marriage. Her mother blamed her father, and her father blamed her mother. Even Kitty, after all this time, couldn't reconcile the people they'd become. It had been a happy family life filled with love. She'd witnessed her parents adore each other...until they hadn't.

Kitty didn't know what had happened to shatter their family, but at age twelve, she became embroiled in her parent's divorce and spent most of her teenage years dumped between houses and the ringmaster of disputes. Now, she had a distant relationship with both of them. Her mother had never recovered and had not re-partnered. Unlike her father, who had gone on to have multiple girlfriends, each of whom she'd met and spent time with until he married the current one. Kitty didn't expect it to last.

So why did she think she was different? Why did she think she could find everlasting love when most people could not? And with such wonderful role models…

The lights of the town flickered in the moonlight.

Remember why you're here Kitty. Forget Stuart and focus on your dream. That was the other thing; Stuart always said he supported her desire to become a perfumer, but it had never happened and it was always within his control. Why hadn't he let her follow her dream?

Didn't matter. She was here, now and would seize the moment. She had to make dazzling perfume. She could, right? She had to persevere.

Yes. Returning to her bedside table, she picked up a thick book, the hard cover depicting an elegant glass bottle. The textbook had been lying around downstairs, and she'd borrowed it.

Kitty opened the cover and commenced to read. The scientific words jumbled in her brain; their meaning was unintelligible to her. She skipped ahead a few pages. Tried again, checked definitions in the back and it still didn't make sense. She was a bit tired. But deep-down Kitty feared it wasn't fatigue, what if she wasn't cut out for this perfume making business. If so, she had nothing.

Chapter Nine

'Let me show you.' Pierre leaned in as close to Kitty as her large-brimmed hat would allow and closer than was strictly necessary. The scent in the field was powerful, but today, his blossoming buds were overwhelmed by Kitty Landers.

She wore a *House of Joubert* scent. It was the first time he hadn't smelled magnolia on her skin, and it pleased him more than he could describe. Trouble was that he wanted to drown himself in it and in her and bathe in the fragrance of Kitty.

She stood wide-eyed next to him in the field amongst the two dozen or so other flower pickers. Like everyone, she wore the white picking apron, gaping open at the moment with its emptiness. Unfortunately for Pierre, it hid her long, lean legs.

'First, you need to determine if the flower is ready. We will pick every day over the next two weeks, and we do that because, today, some flowers are ready to be plucked.' He paused because he lost focus as her rose lips parted. He had to divert his gaze.

'Those that aren't ready today might be ready tomorrow or anytime over the next couple of weeks.'

The floppy brim of her oversized hat moved as she nodded. Pierre was able to focus again when it covered some of her face.

'See here, this one?' He cupped an open flower with gentle care. 'The petals are open, and it appears in bloom, yes?'

'Yep.'

'You place the open flower between your thumb and index finger before picking, and tug. Hear that sound?' He exaggerated his movements and there was the distinct popping noise when the flower came away from the stem. 'You want to hear a nice clean break. And then you place it into your apron and pick the next one until that entire bush is done for today.' Pierre placed the flower into her apron, conscious of how close his hand was to her body. 'Be careful, though, while the bushes are beautiful and filled with green leafy foliage, there are thorns on the stems. Keep your hands to the top. Okay, you show me.'

With great care Kitty chose a flower and picked it.

He smiled. '*Parfait.*'

'What if I pick a flower that isn't ready? Will it be ruined?' Her hands fidgeted.

'You worry too much. It will be fine. Only pick the flowers in blossom, and all will be well. I'll stay with you a while.' It was the only place he wanted to be. They worked in companionable silence until he said. 'You look tired today.'

Kitty didn't stop picking. 'I didn't sleep well last night.'

Pierre regarded her and she replied. 'You look tired, too.'

'Ah, I don't sleep well either...'

Kitty's hands paused around a perfect pink flower head, and

she looked as if she was about to say something when someone approached.

'*Bonjour, Pierre.*' A twinge of disappointment hit Pierre as he turned to Monique. He enjoyed speaking with this beautiful Australian girl, perhaps way too much.

Kitty was gorgeous with her luscious blonde wavy locks, bronzed skin, bright, innocent eyes and careful, deliberate manner. She was kind and considerate, and it would be very, very wrong for him to get involved with her. Pierre didn't date, and he didn't do love; romance wasn't on his agenda. That didn't stop his body from quickening each time she was near. Something unlocked inside him when she smiled, and her whole face lit up, hiding the sadness that sometimes lingered in her eyes. It was that part he was most attracted to, but everyone had a story and he didn't need to know hers to understand Kitty was a romantic, wore her heart on her sleeve and deserved better than him.

Unlike the other pickers, she wore that ridiculous Grace Kelly hat to protect herself from the harsh morning sun, but her hair tumbled loose at its base. He was glad; her lovely blonde hair flowed freely in golden waves.

Monique, with her Mediterranean complexion was as dark as Kitty was blonde.

'Monique, hello,' he replied in English. They cheek-kissed, and she kept her hand on his upper arm, right over his bicep and returned a broad, sultry smile.

'I didn't see you at the club last night? Were you hiding? I missed you.' She trailed her bright red nails down his arm, cocked her knee into a bent position and swivelled her hips forward. Monique was beautiful, and they'd spent one passionate night together a few months ago. It had been a mistake; it always was with him because, like the others, Monique wanted more than he was prepared to offer. Pierre was sure she was only helping with flower harvest today to gain an opportunity for them to spend time together.

It made his heart heavy; it was never his intention to hurt anyone. He always made his intentions clear, but it rarely seemed to matter. He glanced back at Kitty. Would she be the same? All of a sudden, his body came alive with lust as images of their naked bodies coming together played through his head.

No, he shook those pictures away. He couldn't go there.

The pressure on his arm increased.

Pierre reverted to French. 'I was there. I'm sorry we didn't see one another. Next time.'

Monique pouted before she walked away.

Kitty had watched the exchange. As he turned back to the bush, she said, 'This country is full of beautiful people.'

'Well, you are, what you say, a perfect fit then.' He kept working but heard her soft gasp.

As each picker passed his row, they shouted greetings and Pierre kissed the women and offered handshakes and back slaps to the men.

'This is a big event, right? The farm is different to last time I was here. It was so quiet then, and today, it's a hive of activity.'

'Mmm,' he replied.

'Do you know all of these people?'

He looked around him, and the sight made his chest puff out. His fields were filled with people tending to his flowers. The harvest. A year's work and it all came down to this.

'*Oui*, yes. Some are friends and locals; others are seasonal pickers who travel from farm to farm to pick the flowers. Varieties of flowers are harvested at different times, so it works. Many workers return year after year. It is good, they work hard and know what to do.'

'Wow, what a job. Must be wonderful to be surrounded by such beauty every day and the smell!' Kitty bent her head into the bush, and he laughed.

'Can you tell me about this rose? I think it might be my favourite.'

Pierre picked a few more blossoms before replying. Was she for real? Or was she, like everyone else, trying to impress him and get his attention? This town was passionate about perfume; it was in their blood and was what they lived for, but he rarely met anyone who really cared, well, as much as him, anyway. Kitty said she wanted to be a perfumer; maybe she did. So, he told her all he knew about his beloved centifolia rose.

Occasionally, they'd reach for the same bud, and their arms brushed. Surreptitiously she'd glance up, waiting for his reaction. Her eyes were wide, her lips parted.

Oh yes, he noticed the touch and did a great job of hiding the electric jolt that shot straight to his core. Man, he wanted to rip that hat straight off her head and...

Instead, he kept on with his factual monologue, which never seemed to bore her, until a commotion caught his attention to the right, and Buster flew across the top of the field, racing back and forth, much to everyone's delight. Mrs Roubillard chased after him.

Kitty laughed along with everyone else.

'I'd better go and help Mrs Roubillard. Naughty Buster was

meant to be safely secured out the back,' he said. 'I'll see you soon.'

After two hours of picking, Kitty took the opportunity to stretch. The rose bushes were mid-height but the bent-over position was sending her back into spasm.

'It is physical, yes,' Mrs Roubillard said as she approached. 'More hurt the body than you think.'

'That's for sure.' She smiled at the woman as they both watched Pierre encourage the dog away from the fields.

'We have lunch at end of picking today, you must come. I cook.' Mrs Roubillard had resumed Pierre's position next to her in the row of flowers and donned her own apron.

'You do a bit of everything, then?'

The lady's features scrunched in confusion. Kitty gestured towards the bushes. 'You pick flowers, do farm tours, and cook.'

She beamed. 'Yes, everything. I do anything for Pierre.' Her eyes twinkled and her expression became animated. Clearly, there was nothing she wouldn't do for him. Another female to add to his fan club.

'Have you worked here long?'

'Oh, yes, my whole life. I worked for his family before and have known him since he was a baby. I was his nanny and when he grew up and moved out, he kept me on as his housekeeper.'

'It's a beautiful place to live.'

'Yes, it is, and he is a wonderful boss and man.' She turned serious then and faced Kitty. 'Don't let anyone tell you otherwise; don't listen to gossip. Pierre Joubert is a kind and loving man, a generous employer and cares about the people around him. He works very hard. But see, here today,' she pointed to where he stood, 'this is where he is the happiest, on his flower farm.'

Kitty expressed her surprise. 'Here? But he's the CEO of one of the best perfume houses in Grasse and perhaps France...'

'Oh, yes, the world, probably.'

Kitty doubted that because she hadn't heard of them back home, but who was she to argue?

'Yes, but it is the family business. Don't get me wrong.' She patted Kitty's arm. 'He lives for perfume, like everyone here.' She gestured with wide arms. 'And he's good at his job. He runs the company now after his father has stepped down, and he is a perfumer at heart, but it is the flowers he loves the most.' There was no need for a reply, so she continued. 'He works hard, and he plays hard, too but, that means nothing. His heart is here, in this field. With his flowers.'

Kitty scanned the field for Pierre. Warmth flushed her chest as she found him amongst the vines. That dashingly handsome man who had women throwing themselves at him, loved growing flowers more than making perfume? He was one of the most gifted noses in the region! Yes, she understood he had a team to make the perfumes, but she'd imagined that was what he lived for. Like her. So, preferring his flowers seemed a crazy notion to her.

On cue, another gorgeous woman clutched his arm and batted her eyelashes seductively. He didn't pause in his picking. Kitty couldn't tear her gaze away as the muscles in his arms rippled as he moved from bud to bud, his strong legs keeping him balanced. His movement caused a loose lock of curl to flop into his eyes. Pierre ignored it and kept working, his face a study in concentration. Kitty watched him for a beat too long because he glanced up and caught her. Their eyes connected for the briefest moment.

Didn't men like him belong in sports cars and wearing expensive suits attending prestigious celebrity events, not here in old clothes picking flowers?

None of it made sense. What was Mrs Roubillard *really* saying?

Kitty held his gaze, and his lips parted. What would it be like to kiss him? A wave of desire pulsed through her, and she filled with giddy pleasure.

'*Oh, excusez-moi.*' Mrs Roubillard bumped into Kitty, breaking up her daydream. Reluctantly, she turned back to her rose bush. Onto her fourth apron now, and her arms grew heavy. The jute bags were lining up; the day's picking was almost done. 'He is handsome, yes? Better than Australian men?' Mrs Roubillard grinned at her.

Kitty looked at Pierre again and his gaze remained locked on hers. She placed the flower she'd just picked into her apron as little water droplets trickled down between her breasts.

Someone greeted Mrs Roubillard and the moment was broken. Kitty tore her gaze away, focused on the row of bushes, tried to ignore the wild fluttering in the base of her stomach.

Mrs Roubillard robustly kissed a man on both cheeks before he pinched her on the bottom and sauntered away. 'I go and prepare lunch,' she said, her face rosy. 'You come when you finish this row.'

Kitty agreed but then looked to her right. Far out! The row hadn't seemed so long this morning, but damn it, she could do it. The seasoned pickers stood under the shade of a tree, smoking cigarettes and drinking cool drinks, having already finished. She could do this. Kitty puffed out her cheeks and got on with it.

***

Kitty shuffled into the shed, her feet barely lifting. She was the last to arrive. The pickers sat at long plank tables and their merriment as they ate and drank was deafening.

The French sure knew how to enjoy themselves. They seemed to do a lot of things right.

Before she'd found a place to sit, Mrs Roubillard offered her both a cold glass of water and a delightfully dark wine that sloshed over the glass rim as she placed it on the table. Kitty gulped the water and watched the red stain bleed across the white tablecloth. A shooting ache spiralled up her arm as she reached for the wine flute. Every muscle burned.

Grateful, Kitty allowed Mrs Roubillard to serve her with pasta and bread.

The first bite restored some energy and her spirits lifted as she tuned into her surroundings. A deep honey-throated laugh barrelled across the room and she looked up between mouthfuls of lasagne to see a lady collapse into Pierre's lap. Pierre threw his head back as he held her around the waist. The woman was dressed in high wedges and an emerald summer dress with bare shoulders. Hardly the attire for flower picking.

'Oh, do you see what she's wearing?' Kitty eavesdropped on the conversation at her table where five other women sat and thankfully, they spoke English. Eyes zeroed in on Pierre. 'I mean, good luck to her. Today is her lucky day, everyone gets to have their turn, don't they? Pierre is a dreamboat but he's happy to share the love around. A different girl each week, sometimes more than one.'

The group of women murmured their agreement as they watched the flirtation. The woman on Pierre's lap swished her long mahogany locks around in a seductive fashion revealing milky white skin. Kitty wasn't sure whether she envied the woman's looks or her chosen seat.

'The problem is every woman thinks they can change him and be *the* one. It's a trap and bullshit ladies, let's agree. But if I'm ever feeling lonely for some loving, I know where to look, but he'll never offer anything more.'

The women cheered each other in solidarity as Mrs Roubillard arrived to collect their dirty plates. 'Are you finished, ladies?'

Her tone was curt. Had she overheard? Chastised, the group drank the last remnants of their wine and stood to leave. Pierre called his thanks and gratitude and that he'd see them tomorrow.

Mrs Roubillard sat down next to her, and the handsome man from earlier joined them.

The housekeeper's eyes sparkled and the smile lifted from her mouth to brighten her entire face. 'Is this your husband?' Kitty asked.

They laughed together before Mrs Roubillard placed her hand on Kitty's knee under the table. 'He's my lover.'

Kitty spluttered out the sip of wine she'd just taken and wiped her mouth with a cloth serviette. 'Pardon?'

'Andreas is married with a family. He is what you call, my *paramour* but lover suits best.'

'Um, okay.' It was hardly a suitable reply but she struggled to form her words.

Mrs Roubillard chortled and gripped her knee firmer. 'It's okay, my love. It is not uncommon here, and I understand that Andreas has a wife. It suits me. I do not wish to leave Pierre or have my own family, so the arrangement is perfect. When we see each other, it is passionate and hot, and we have fantastic sex.'

A lump caught in Kitty's throat, and she coughed. She watched the woman's hand lift from her leg to caress the arm of Andreas who gazed at her with adoration.

But what about his wife?

'If you adore each other, don't you always want to be together? Without competing interests?' They were being honest, and so she would be, too.

Mrs Roubillard released a soft sigh and paused to collect her thoughts before she spoke. The weight of the pause felt like pity at her lack of understanding, and in that moment, Kitty felt very inexperienced.

'I love Andreas, and if the only way we can be together is to snatch precious moments of time, I will accept that. I do not demand anything from him.'

In a flash Kitty went from feeling stupid to the feminist in her raging against this position. Especially as Andreas sat back, seemingly amused. Kitty gave him a loaded stare.

'I know what you're thinking, mademoiselle. That I am an adulterer, but I love my wife, and I love Marie; they are both special to me.'

And damn it, the way he gazed at Mrs Roubillard, Kitty could almost forgive him. No man had ever looked at her like that. So perhaps she didn't know anything after all. Love could take all forms, right? However, even being sworn off love, she didn't think she'd take second fiddle to another woman anytime soon.

Andreas and Marie rose together and served platters of cheese to each table. The crowd dwindled, and Kitty sat alone, enjoying a late afternoon coffee. Her head rested in her hand; the weight heavy as fatigue hit her.

A soft hand landed on her shoulder. 'You are exhausted, my love; go home and get some rest.'

Fairy godmother, Mrs Roubillard, tugged her to her feet. Kitty checked for Pierre, but the shed was empty. Disappointment flooded through her but as she swung her leg over the bench seat, she realised her body ached from the tip of her toes to her neck. It had seized up while she'd been sitting for lunch. Riding home would be torture.

Mrs Roubillard kissed her on each cheek in farewell.

Chapter Ten

Despite her exhaustion, Kitty arrived back at the Villa, hardly having raised a sweat.

'*Ma Cherie*!' Adrienne exclaimed when she entered. 'This arrived for you this afternoon by personal delivery.' The house mistress held aloft a cream envelope.

'For me?' Her first thought was Stuart, and she immediately hated herself for it.

The beaming faces of the loving couple who had become her surrogate parents waited expectantly. She guessed she wouldn't be opening the letter in private.

Kitty ripped open the envelope and extracted a small piece of cream card with gold embossed writing. 'It's an invitation,' she said as she scanned the words. Probably because of the ruckus caused by the house masters, some of the other guests wandered in. Great, a bigger audience to ridicule her.

Adrienne flapped her arms around in an agitated manner. 'Don't keep us in suspense, an invitation to what?'

'To a private event to showcase the perfumes of *Beaumont de Villiers* tonight at 7 p.m. at *La Mairie*...' Kitty looked up quizzically.

'The town hall,' Raph translated.

'*Oh, la*! Who invited you, hey? Your handsome teacher?' One of the students surmised.

'There's no name on the card, but I presume it's Henri. Perhaps he invited the class?'

'Betcha he didn't. Got eyes for you, has he?' said Julia, the British blonde. Her lascivious tone made Kitty immediately uncomfortable and her defences ignited.

'No, he hasn't. I'm sure all the students are invited. He's very generous with his knowledge.'

'What's the dress code?' asked Sofia who always looked glamorous with her designer clothes and perfectly coiffured hair and manicured nails.

Kitty picked up the card again. 'Cocktail. Bugger. The only fancy outfit I brought was my wedding dress and I threw that in the bin at the railway station.'

'You what?' asked Henrietta. The mouths of the women hung open.

'You were getting married, *ma cherie*?' Adrienne asked.

Kitty sighed. Guess she had to spill the beans now. 'Yes. I was getting married, and I was ready to walk down the aisle when my fiancé dumped me by text message.'

A collective gasp filled the air.

'Then I hopped straight on our honeymoon flight, except unfortunately, it took me to Paris. I couldn't stand to be in the city of love after being jilted, and I hightailed it out of there as fast as I could and came here instead. I wore my wedding dress on the plane until Singapore and then nursed it until I threw it in the garbage when I arrived in Grasse.'

'*Wow.*' '*Bastard.*' '*Pig.*' '*How could he?*' were the cries from the girls. Adrienne drew her in for a hug.

'I'll do your hair for tonight,' said Sofia.

'I'll do your makeup,' said Julia.

What?

Wow, now she was gobsmacked. All it took was a story of heartbreak and joined solidarity over men for these girls to like her. Perhaps they'd been heartbroken too? Maybe she should have been honest from the start?

'And you can rummage around in my wardrobe, I'm sure we'll find something *magnifique* to wear. We are about the same size, and you know, I used to go out a bit.' Adrienne smiled and Raph backed up the sentiment.

'After we're finished with you, we'll take a photo and send it to the Australian man who dumped you. He will be sorry,' gushed Henrietta in her clipped English.

The group laughed.

'Hey, what's so funny?' asked Chad as he entered.

'Kitty has a date!' they chorused.

***

Kitty stood outside *la mairie* and loosened the straps of her borrowed stilettos. It was only a short walk from her accommodation but still her feet ached. No bike riding tonight!

The soft lulling music drifted down towards her as she stood at the base of a grand, stone staircase. In the centre of the village, the town hall was a stunning building of traditional tangerine muted orange brick that stood multiple storeys high. She saw signs for the tourist office—which would have been handy when she first arrived—and for parliamentary offices. Kitty was pretty sure the few people floating up the stairs were dressed for a party.

Her beautiful cream clutch, borrowed from Adrienne, vibrated with an incoming notification to her phone, and she took it out. True to their word, the other students at the villa had groomed her until she didn't recognise herself in the mirror. As promised, they'd also taken shots before she left. They'd insisted, and been very persuasive, that she upload a photograph to social media when she refused to send one to Stuart. She hadn't posted online since...well...since she'd left, and her friends at home were delighted to hear from her and were punching out comments and posting every available emoji. It was nice to have a connection with home; she'd chat with them later.

Despite being out of her comfort zone, it was nice to dress up. Adrienne was right; she'd had a few gowns, and the difficulty had been choosing the right one. In the end, she'd chosen a strapless, dark navy sequined dress that reached her knees. Sofia had blown-dry her already-there curls into soft waterfalls around her face. Julia had applied deep russet eye shadow that offset her blonde hair and accentuated her fine features. The shoes, like the clutch, were cream.

Bolstered by the commentary on her feed, it helped her remember where she was and why. She could do this; she could enter this party alone in a foreign country. Fact was, no one knew her anyway. She hurried up the stairs and her mouth gaped open as she reached the top step.

Yellow lighting highlighted the historic building in an orange glow. Two waiters stood like sentries at the imposing, wide entrance and welcomed her with a drink. She snatched that first glass of champagne and sipped it to settle the butterflies taking flight in her tummy.

After collecting her empty flute, they waved her inside, and the first thing that struck her was the sign. Large, bold and white plastic it read *Lys Blancs – the best in French scent.* Pictures of lily flowers surrounded the words. Entering, a powderpuff of scent engulfed her, seeping into her pores and becoming the only thing she could smell. There was nothing subtle about this fragrance; it was strong, and Kitty forced down a cough and covered her mouth. Lilies covered every available surface, beautiful with their long, white petals. But it was the distinct scent of musk or wood, or perhaps sandalwood, that didn't quite fit and stifled the delicious scent of the flowers hiding underneath. The fizz of the champagne kept popping and Kitty collected another drink, choosing to inhale that aroma instead.

Soft music played from speakers positioned in each corner of the spacious room. The room was large, obviously the main banquet hall, but at a guess, she'd say fifty or so people were present. A more prominent group of patrons gathered in the centre, and she wandered over. Flashlights popped, and she observed Henri standing with an older gentleman and two young men talking to what she assumed was the press. Three men had cameras around their necks and notepads in their hands. A model dressed in white with gold jewellery stood with them and posed, holding a bunch of lilies.

From the odd words she caught, *lys blancs*, meant white lilies. Pretty fitting, she figured, given they were in a valley and lily flowers adorned many of the fields. Henri saw her and winked. He was busy so she wandered away towards a display.

A paisley cloth covered a table with the signature perfume of the night. The lower half of the glass bottle matched the paisley print, and the top half was clear with a silver twist on the top lid. There were various sizes and varieties: eau de toilettes, eau du parfum and perfume. At the end stood a black bottle labelled cologne. Surely not of the same scent? Using one of the provided blotter strips, she sprayed and sniffed. It was heavier on the musk and sandalwood, with almond, but it was the same combination of elements. A version for men. Kitty wrinkled her nose.

'Tell me the top notes.' The voice was deep and sensual and sent a ripple of awareness through her, anchoring her to the spot.

She answered without turning around. 'The heart notes.' She rattled them off. 'The base notes.' Turning then, she faced Pierre, their bodies deliciously close.

'Extraordinary,' he murmured. Her eyes lifted to his. Those clear ice-blue ink pools turned dark and simmered with intensity. She could read desire as his gaze slid to her lips. Kitty sensed it wasn't her perfume skill that had this effect on him, and the prospect that Pierre Joubert found her alluring sent waves of pleasant heat through her body.

She waited a heartbeat, tilted her head. 'Am I right?'

Pierre ran his tongue across his lips before replying. 'You know you are.'

And honestly, she could have ravished him then.

'What do you think of this scent by Beaumont?' Tiny creases appeared at the corners of his eyes as if he held in his amusement.

He stood so close, she couldn't think. She jumbled her words at first but then managed to speak coherently. 'It's a little heavy on the sandalwood, which makes it quite musky and woody. I like lighter and fresher with less spice.' Finding her groove, she stared hard at him in challenge.

He didn't reply, his eyes remained transfixed on her.

'What do you think?' she whispered.

Instead of answering, he jutted his chin. Her eyes roamed his face, down his body to his feet, before glancing back up again. His white collared shirt was open at the neck, exposing a smattering of dark chest hair. A red pocket square was the only colour in his otherwise black suit. Damn, he was beautiful.

Kitty swallowed.

His silence racketed up her nerves.

'What are you doing here? This is an event for *Beaumont de Villiers*. Aren't they your sworn enemy?' she blurted out.

His stance relaxed. 'It's not like that.' His voice was liquid honey now. 'We are rivals, yes, competitors, yes. But Grasse is small, and the industry is tiny. We support each other, plus,' he leaned in, 'they are so traditionalist, they never release anything new. This perfume has been done a thousand times in various forms, they simply rebrand and readvertise and promote it as new. The *House of Joubert* is leaps and bounds ahead of them.' His grin was irresistible.

A tray of salmon hors d'oeuvres was served, and Kitty took one, popped it into her mouth, and grimaced.

Pierre smiled. 'Not to your liking?'

'Not so much,' was the best she could offer before draining her glass.

A woman appeared beside Pierre and clasped his elbow. She had blood-red lipstick that contoured her full lips. The lipstick complimented her black dress, which had a full skirt that swished when she moved and displayed sparkling gems along the hemline. Adding to the effect, the fabric had minuscule red roses across her decolletage.

'*Bonjour.*' She addressed Kitty and held out her other hand to shake but didn't offer her name. Despite being dressed differently tonight, Kitty still recognised her. The woman from the train station. Was she Pierre's regular companion or tonight's lucky prize?

'Your show is soon, yes, Pierre?' she asked him.

He was fast to correct her. 'It's not a show. It's the launch of our latest fragrance next week in Monaco. Ms Landers, you must come.'

Was that a demand or a request?

'Is it invitation only?'

'Of course.' His body stiffened and the air around them shifted. Had she offended him?

The woman finished her champagne.

'Would you like another?' Pierre asked extracting himself from her grip. After her confirmation, he asked Kitty the same.

'Yes, please. But we can simply wait for a waiter, can't we?'

'The first glass is complimentary; the rest are paid for at the bar.'

'I can get myself a drink.'

'I'm sure you can, but I'd be delighted,' he said.

His companion waved to someone across the room and walked off. Pierre headed towards the bar, and be damned if she could shift her gaze from his disappearing physique. Her mind fast-forwarded. Would Pierre leave tonight with that woman? Were the rumours true? But she'd seen him with this lady at least twice. That defied convention. And what about what Mrs

Roubillard said? Perhaps he dated some women and slept with others? The questions spiralled like a fast-flowing stream as another presence sidled up next to her.

———

Henri kissed her in his trademark gesture. He leaned in to speak, but a thumping bass filled the room after the previous mellow song and drowned out his words. Instead, he dazzled her with a cheeky grin before tugging her into the middle of the dance floor. A gap in the crowd allowed her to spot Pierre at the bar, entwined around another elegant woman.

Oh no, she was a terrible dancer and had failed ballroom as a kid!

They circled the floor, Henri holding her firmly in his arms. His formal suit was stiff against her and the *Lys Blancs* cologne clogged her nose and she sneezed. Despite his clammy palm in her grip, his feet moved to the beat, and she was swept along with him. After a few stumbles, they developed a rhythm and glided together effortlessly.

So, Henri could be spontaneous. And he liked to dance? She'd never have guessed.

After a change in song, other dancers entered the floor. With each twist and turn, she caught fleeting glimpses of Pierre in the crowd.

'You look stunning this evening and are the belle of my ball. Thank you for coming and being here with me.' The music stopped and they stood close. Her instinct was to turn away and catch her breath. But guests surrounded them speaking to each other and making introductions. Henri's family joined in. The number of relatives surprised her; there was a lot of them! She'd only ever thought of him as one entity. Strange.

Kitty joined Henri's family as they spilled onto the outdoor balcony, where fewer people congregated and the cool night air kissed her skin.

'You make a lovely couple,' his grandmother said. 'Isn't he handsome?' She tilted her head in Henri's direction where he stood talking to one of his sisters. 'He will make a wonderful husband. He's kind, caring and considerate.' Was Grandma reading his Tinder profile?

Why wasn't Henri married if she was such a catch? Kitty mused but she nodded at the grandmother, not quite able to trust her voice.

'Are you looking for a husband? Is that why you're in Grasse?'

Kitty longed for a drink. Her throat was dry, plus it would buy her time to construct a response. Was the old lady serious? She couldn't be right? This was the twenty-first century. But she was such a dear thing with her cherub cheeks with too much rouge, bright pink lipstick and a floral frock. She was a head shorter than Kitty, who looked down upon her.

'I'm here to become a perfumer,' Kitty used the French pronunciation.

The woman laughed, her face extenuating her already present wrinkles. 'Oh, my dear, that's for the men. The generations of men who've learned the trade from their fathers before them. It's not something for women to learn, you are born to it, it's in your genes.' She petted her on the arm in a patronising manner as if she'd get over her crazy notion.

'But what of your granddaughters? Will they not continue the tradition?'

'Of course! It's a family business and they'll balance the books, run the shop, design the pretty labels, and perform marketing and HR. Most importantly they will wear the perfume. There is plenty to do.'

'And if they want to create beautiful perfume?'

'They will not make it for *Beaumont de Villiers*.'

'For another perfume house then? There are many in Grasse, in France?'

'It is an industry based on tradition. Women are not destined to create. Creation is men's work. Women are the embodiment of the creation and,' she nodded conspiratorially, 'if you are careful, you could become part of something great here.'

Henri's grandmother morphed into Ursula out of the children's fairy tale *The Little Mermaid*. Kitty wanted to get away from her and her old-fashioned ideas. Wanted to escape from the smell of lilies that was now making her nauseous. She turned on her heel and walked past Henri and his family, past the dwindling crowd. Near the exit, she bumped into Pierre, who was standing with a woman on each arm. As she strode past, she registered the flicker of concern that crossed his face. Urgh, she didn't want to see him either. That man could not keep his hands to himself. Like Cinderella fleeing from the ball at midnight, Kitty raced down the grand staircase. At the base, she removed her shoes, letting them dangle from her hand as she disappeared into the black night.

Chapter Eleven

With scratchy eyes and a mind foggy with lack of sleep, Pierre watched Kitty work as the morning sped by. Her movements were jerky, rushed, her body stiff. She'd gotten straight into picking and she hadn't paused since. Her arrival at the farm in the early hours of the dawning day had been like a spectacular sunrise, making the whole world shine around her. Particularly after the night he'd had. By mid-morning her upper lip glistened with moisture.

He stood behind her as she worked harvesting his precious blooms. He breathed her in before taking a step back. Traces of *Lys Blancs* clung to her skin and hair. He'd had enough of that scent last night.

'You came back,' he said.

'Yes.' Kitty took a deep sniff of the bloom in her hand before placing it into her apron and stretching out her back. 'You look dreadful. Again. Big night?' She crossed her arms and stared at him. Her cheeks were flushed and her lips were set in a straight line.

Something was wrong. Was she angry at him? And why? She was damn cute nonetheless. 'Not as big as yours.' He retaliated with a smouldering smile.

Kitty placed her hands on her hips, feet apart. 'Don't be ridiculous. I had a very civilised evening. Unlike yours, I suspect.'

Pierre frowned but Kitty barrelled on.

'What did you get up to?' Then she threw her arms in the air. 'No! Don't answer that. I don't care. You can do whatever you like and with whomever you like.'

'Why did you rush away?' he asked.

Kitty remained silent.

'Did something happen?'

'Did something happen? Well, let's see. I spent years in a relationship where I thought I was loved and then am ceremoniously dumped. And before that I dutifully work in a shop selling perfume for a renowned company on a promise that one day, I'll be allowed to make the perfume. But then I'm no longer engaged and no longer employed, and I flee across the world to learn the trade I've always dreamed about. But I have no chemical qualifications, and everyone thinks I'm a joke, and then ... then, it seems as if the French treat their women as objects and as otherwise useless beings who cannot make gainful contributions to life.'

Pierre continued to frown. Was she being sarcastic? Kitty took a deep breath and continued.

'Are all Frenchmen misogynists, only interested in keeping trophy wives chained to the sink and to clean their house?'

What on earth was she talking about? Being chained to a sink? But Kitty still wasn't finished. 'Why do you have a house-keeper, Pierre? Aren't you capable of cleaning your own toilet and making your meals and doing your laundry?'

'Mrs Roubillard is much more to me than hired help...'

'Is she?' A snarky tone entered her voice.

He tapped his foot and counted to five, trying to keep up with the conversation and failing. 'I'm not sure what you mean. Mrs Roubillard is my friend. She has been part of my family since I was a baby. She was no longer required after I was an adult, and she would have been unemployed and homeless. Then I bought this house. In fact, I offered to let her live here for free in a separate cottage with her own facilities, but she insisted on caring for me and the house. She's like a mother to me.' He didn't add that she was the only adult who loved him. That would sound pathetic.

Kitty dropped her arms. 'Do you hire and train female noses at your perfume house?'

'Yes, they are some of our best.' Pierre rubbed his hands down his face, tired, unsure. Was he being accused of something?

'Papa Pierre!' A boy shrieked and hugged him around his legs.

His heart jumped into his throat and he knelt to the boy's level. 'Claude? Are you feeling better?' He placed the back of his hand to the boy's forehead.

'Yes, *merci*, much better. The medicine you bought really worked. I'm a little tired now but very excited to help you harvest your beautiful flowers.' Pierre ruffled the boy's hair before a group of children descended upon him.

Ms Dubois followed. '*Les enfants!*' She sang and Kitty gasped. The teacher was trying to gain control of the rambunctious group of children, but they were too excited. Out of the corner of his eye, Pierre watched Kitty swing her gaze between him and Ms Dubois. Now it was her turn to frown.

Pierre clapped his hands and the children quietened and looked at him. Listen, children! Let's have a cool drink and you can wash your hands and we'll assign you to a picker who will help you today.' They cheered and jostled and like always, his rough edges melted away. Their joy was like a rainbow after a storm. Kitty still stared, her lips parted, but with the children calm now, Ms Dubois was able to regain control.

'Melodie, may I please introduce...' he paused. Friend? Acquaintance? He didn't know what to call Kitty, and instead, opted for her name. 'Kitty Landers from Australia. She is here helping me pick and has an amazing talent for scent.'

Kitty turned to face him. 'Kitty, this is Ms Melodie Dubois, she is the new teacher at the local home where these children live.'

A thousand questions flittered across Kitty's eyes. He'd answer them later.

'Papa Pierre.' Claude tugged on his long-sleeved shirt.

'*Oui*, Claude?'

'Can I help the pretty lady?' he pointed to Kitty, who blushed under the attention. Trust Claude to pick out the best. Kitty was back to being the innocent and bright-natured girl he knew. He thought back on her comments and was baffled. She thought she was a joke? The French don't like women? She was engaged and now she's not. They had much to discuss.

He smiled at Claude. 'Claude, may I introduce you to Kitty.

Kitty would it be all right if Claude worked alongside you this morning? You picked last year, didn't you, Claude? Do you remember how?'

Most of the children from the home were new to this experience. Not Claude. He'd been at the home long enough to experience three birthdays and Christmas and last year's harvest. The smaller children were always adopted first, the cute factor, he called it. Claude had so much to offer but at ten he couldn't compete with babies and toddlers. That familiar ache hit Pierre square in the chest. If his brother was alive.... No. Not now. Not today. He bolstered his resolve. Regardless, he'd always care for Claude and any other child that needed him.

Kitty's voice brought him back to the present. 'I would love to harvest with Claude.'

After a long, hot morning. Melodie Dubois sat down beside Kitty at the bench table in the shed to eat her lunch. Today, there was another fine spread; it seemed as if every meal the French ate was a celebration. And, she guessed, today it was also a feast for the children and their hard work. It seemed if anyone deserved fine food and some fun, it was these kids.

Claude had been very talkative on their stretch of picking, excepting about his own background and how he came to be at the home. Not shy of other topics, though, he'd chatted about Pierre. Pierre this, Pierre that; the boy adored "Papa Pierre" who it appeared might be the only male in his life. But he'd also been a wealth of information. Claude told Kitty that Pierre owned the home where he lived and looked after the children. Was this place an orphanage? When asking Claude to explain further, he'd said that Papa Pierre visited them, provided gifts, their food and teachers and a safe and comfortable place to live.

Was Claude talking about the same Pierre? Kitty turned her gaze across the room to catch him smiling mischievously at a little girl sitting next to him and playing one of those handshake games while reciting a rhyme. What else didn't she know about this mysterious Frenchman?

So, when Melodie sat down, Kitty pumped her for further information before she'd eaten her first forkful. 'You work as a teacher at the home?'

Melodie chewed before replying. 'At *Maison de Roses,* yes.'

'Claude said that the older children attend classes at the local school, so where does that leave room for a teacher? It's not a school?'

Melodie nodded. 'Yes, the children attend school but because of their diverse backgrounds, some are behind in their learning, so I help them with homework and additional studies. Tutoring is a better word and for the smaller children, I commence teaching their letters and numbers and basic reading as early as possible to give them a head start.'

'What are their diverse backgrounds?'

Melodie considered her answer before replying. 'Usually, they are at the home because they have no family to care for them, but often it's because of abuse that has meant they cannot live at home.'

'That is terrible,' Kitty said under her breath. A whole range of scenarios flickered through her mind, and a shiver raced up her spine.

'*Oui, c'est vraiment.* Some of them are disturbed, have nightmares, do not eat properly, experience trauma. There is a counsellor on staff too, and in this role, it's often all hands-on deck, so to speak. Helping out wherever needed.'

'And, Pierre, this Pierre...' Kitty pointed to across the room. 'He owns it?' Her voice took on an incredulous tone.

Melodie nodded again. 'Yes, he funds the entire operation, pays my wages and the other staff, all of the expenses and running costs.'

Well, the man was a barrel of surprises. It was obvious Pierre was rich. Look at his house. And he was the CEO of a very successful family company...so it seemed he had the resources. And, of course, that dash of arrogance thrown in would come in good stead. He was a conundrum...he had an austere air about him but never acted entitled, but rather seemed like a normal guy. But if he was excessively wealthy, he had an obligation to help those less fortunate, didn't he? But what drove him to help these children? A thousand questions popped into Kitty's head as she nibbled on some cheese.

'He's so much more than simply the owner, though. Last night Claude was sick. We received a call whilst we were at the event and without any hesitation, Pierre left and spent the night with him. Firstly, getting him the medical treatment he needed but then staying with him through the night. As any parent would.'

Melodie stared at her intently. Perhaps to ensure she understood the gravity of the words and her intended meaning? Kitty swallowed and the food in her mouth went down as a hard lump. 'Why would he do that?'

Melodie shrugged as if the answer was obvious. 'Haven't you seen him with them? He adores them like his own children. He behaves as if he is the only responsible adult they have. As if he caused their circumstances; as if he is trying to make recompense for the awful things that have happened to them. He loves them.'

Kitty was lost for words. What he was doing was indescribable to her. Beyond any words that she could find suitable. Beyond selfless. Her gaze moved across the room once more to watch him.

Pierre was kind. She could vouch for that. Kitty had witnessed it this morning. He'd been wonderful with the children. More patient than any parent would have been. Ready to listen at their level, talked to them with care and compassion, showed interest with many attempts to keep them engaged. It was something she'd only ever seen from devoted parents.

Even now he sat at a table surrounded by little people whom he kept in hysterics by playing games. He was being *silly, childish, and fun.*

'It was lovely being dressed up last night. Did you have a good time?' Melodie asked.

Kitty had Melodie all wrong and was happy to admit it. She was nice. 'Uh huh, it was my first French party.' She paused to collect her thoughts. 'How is it that you accompanied Pierre? I mean, he's your boss...'. Kitty didn't want to fish for gossip but she was desperate to know the nature of their relationship.

Melodie's eyes sparkled and her voice rose in pitch while she inched forward in her seat. 'It was so kind of him. I think he saw it as some sort of treat, you know, for working hard. I'm new to town as well and don't know many people. Why were you there?'

'Oh, I attend the *Ecole du Beau Parfum*.' Melodie's face

scrunched up. 'It's a perfume school run by Henri Beaumont who was holding the event.'

'Were you his date?' she smiled.

'No!' Kitty responded with more force than she intended. However, she didn't want there to be any misunderstandings. But then, again, hadn't she been Henri's date? Never mind, she still felt the need to deny the fact.

The children finished their food and were becoming playful and noisy. 'What's happening?' she asked as Melodie twisted in her seat to get a better view.

'Pierre has promised them an afternoon of outdoor games, er, football, you know, with a round ball.' The children screeched in excitement as they raced from the room. 'I'd better assist,' she said as she stood. 'Nice talking with you, Kitty.'

The room was quiet now. Kitty felt its emptiness keenly as she stood.

Where was Mrs Roubillard? She always seemed to be hovering nearby. Perhaps she was with her lover? Kitty smiled despite herself. She cleared and piled the dishes high on a table to be carried to the kitchen later. Her eyes lifted unconsciously to the rear of the room and towards Pierre's lab off to the side. Yes, that's exactly where she wanted to be. It was almost as if the room called to her. Without hesitation, she headed towards it. After all, it was Sunday, and she had nowhere else to go.

Inside was set up as if still in use, everything available to her. Dozens of vials of essences and other paraphernalia. Perfect for experimenting and trying out new ideas. Kitty couldn't wait to get started.

Chapter Twelve

The next morning, before picking, Pierre was already in the lab when Kitty entered.

'Tell me about this essence.' He placed his hand on her bare arm. Her skin was cool, and the connection sent a jolt of pure ecstasy straight to his core. Kitty gazed at his hand as if it had the same effect on her, but she pulled away.

He held up the small ten-millilitre vial. 'Tell me about it.' he repeated.

Kitty blushed a bright red and right then, he wanted to kiss her. He wanted to trace his lips down her creamy, pale throat, along her collarbone and chin, forming a trail to that soft mouth. He pressed his lips together to control the urge.

'I was thinking of a time when I was happy and...in love.' He nodded, encouraging her to continue. She turned away seemingly embarrassed. He noticed her tanned and bare shoulders and imagined running his lips along her skin. 'It was the day the man I loved asked me to marry him. There were flowers in a glorious garden providing the most delicious scent, green grass that had not long been cut, children squealing on swings nearby, birds chirping in overhead gum trees and the sun was shining brightly. It was a perfect summer's day. I was flushed with love and exhilaration that my life was secure and safe, and perhaps I had captured what my parents had failed to do.'

Pierre shut down at the talk of love and happy yearnings. There was no denying he wanted to feel the curves of Kitty's body against his hands, her smooth skin under his mouth, run his fingers through her hair...but that was lust. This woman wanted to be loved.

Reality slapped him in the face and his desire evaporated with it.

Focus on the essence. 'I can smell those things.'

Her eyes lit up and her lips formed a perfect "O". Those damn kissable lips. His eyes traced over her face.

'You can?' Her tone was incredulous.

'It's not perfect, but I can tell it has a story, that there was a purpose to it. It is not like your previous attempts that were a melting pot of different ideas mashed together.'

'It came from here.' He pointed to her chest, which rose and fell rapidly. Pierre diverted his gaze from the swell of her breasts, obvious in the singlet top she wore.

'I'm sorry for what happened to you. You mentioned yesterday that you were, what you say, jilted. I understand that means a man broke up with you. I'm sorry. He is very foolish.' She peered up at him then, her eyes glistening. 'I do not know what has happened to you since you've been in Grasse and why you say people think you are funny.'

She bit the corner of her lip as she tended to do when thinking.

'Is it Henri who thinks you are funny?'

Kitty shook her head but didn't elaborate.

Seconds passed. The tension between them became electric. The moment their eyes locked, he knew. He knew he couldn't resist her in this moment. Pierre took one step closer. In movements that felt like slow motion, he cupped her face and kissed her. It was an explosion of senses, of taste and touch. Their mouths moved together with urgency. Kitty moaned and he increased the pressure of his kiss. She held the base of his neck with one hand, her other at his waist. She tasted just as exquisite as he'd imagined and he savoured her sweet, berry taste...

'What the heck?' The unfamiliar voice carried a bold twang.

Kitty jumped back, releasing him.

The American beamed with amusement, moving his stare from one to the other.

Pierre wiped his hands down the front of his shorts and turned away slightly to avoid detection of his arousal.

'Sorry to interrupt.' The man cleared his throat and flashed a wide grin in their direction which seemed to indicate he was anything but sorry. 'So,' he elongated the word. 'This is why you're so committed to harvesting the rose centifolia.' He chuckled, and the tone sounded sinister to Pierre. Another man and two younger women followed him into the room. 'We thought we'd check out flower harvesting, too. Got to learn about the source, right?'

Kitty cleared her throat, too. 'Pierre. This is Chad, along with Pete, Sofia and Julia, they are staying with me at the villa and studying at the Institute.'

Pierre could read Kitty's body language. Her skin was flushed, her hair slightly tussled, and her hands were in her short pockets. These were the students who thought Kitty was a joke, and she was intimidated by them. Gerard, an experienced perfumer and teacher stood behind them. Pierre knew him well, and they greeted each other.

'Okay if I show this lot around your farm and set up?' Gerard asked.

'*Bien sur,* Gerard, of course. It would be my pleasure.'

Kitty checked her wristwatch. 'I've gotta run. I'm late for class.' Pierre watched her walk out, her petite bottom swaying and long lean legs on display in her shorts. Instead of his desire waning, it burned.

On Tuesday, Kitty hesitated when Henri insisted on taking her for dinner after class. 'I miss you,' he'd said. So she hadn't refused and he'd taken her acquiescence for agreement.

Her thoughts focused on Pierre as Henri kissed her hand. 'I've missed you,' he repeated.

Ever since she'd kissed Pierre her lips had burned for more. The recollection of his mouth and hands upon hers still caused her body to erupt in tingles.

The sensual kiss had sent Kitty into a spiral. Afterwards she'd decided to enjoy a holiday romance with Pierre. A thrilling summer liaison with a handsome Frenchman. He was doing it with everyone else, so why not her? It was every girl's dream, right?

Did she only want Pierre for a bout of jaw-dropping lusty

sex? She wasn't sure, but even the thought of it had her hot and bothered. Maybe it was exactly what she needed? Might it cure her of any further romantic notions she carried? That hadn't been knocked out of her after being dumped.

Henri stroked his thumb along the top of her hand and gazed at her with a saccharine smile.

Or maybe an affair with Henri?

He was also a handsome Frenchman. There was nothing stopping her. He liked her! It seemed as if anything was acceptable in France. Take Mrs Roubillard. Yes, but she did find that arrangement scandalous and...and *wrong*. So, maybe not like her.

It was obvious Pierre had an aversion to commitment, so he was perfect. A love affair with no strings attached. Even thinking the words made Kitty itch. She might have to grow into the idea. Deep down she worried she'd lost the plot. Such thoughts were unlike her, but that was exactly the point!

But she had to be able to carry it off...

She returned Henri's smile. He was nothing like Pierre. Henri was the solid, reliable, man that a good girl like her would marry. Once they were characteristics that were very important to her. What good had that done? Now, she thought they were exactly what she didn't want.

Pierre was dangerous and stopped her heart from beating when he gazed at her, when his eyes sank to take in her lips or brush her hair behind her ears.

But Henri was chivalrous. He kissed hands. Yes, he was old-fashioned. He also opened doors and paid her undivided attention. Plus, they'd kissed; they might only be warming up.

'I'd love to have dinner with you.'

'Wonderful.' He clapped his hands together and gave a cheeky, lop-sided grin. 'Let's go now.' He reached for her hand.

The class had finished later than usual, and dusk provided a warm, pink glow over the town. Kitty never tired of looking at the colours, the muted tangerines and oranges mixed in with the dusty pink of the sky continued to take her breath away. This had always been her favourite time of the day. The intense heat of the afternoon had lifted, and the air was less oppressive. Locals had finished work and enjoyed a late afternoon aperitif or sat on fountain rims in the main square chatting with friends. Henri clasped her hand as they walked. It felt natural.

After a short stroll, they arrived at a hotel, *Le Vieux Chateau*, which had an outdoor dining area. Unlike some of the other buildings, this hotel had smaller stonework, like pebbles she'd imagine on a footpath, but tall, broad walls with white shutters and gables on the tiled roof. One façade was covered with creeping vines. 'The Old Castle,' she mumbled. 'It looks like a castle.'

'Food is first class, too,' Henri replied. He opted for sitting on the terrace and held out a chair for her. From that position, she had a clear view overlooking the township.

Champagne arrived without their request and she sipped gratefully.

'Thank you for attending our premier event. I hope you had a nice time.'

'It was wonderful, thank you. It was nice to meet your family. What do they do in the business?'

'My father and brothers are creators. My sisters manage the business side of the company: public relations, advertising and marketing.'

'Your sisters don't create perfumes?' She had to find out from him.

'No, they are not *le nez*,' he said matter-of-factly.

'Did they want to be?' she continued.

He paused. 'I don't think so.'

'Henri, if they had wanted to be *le nez*, would they have been allowed?'

'Of course,' he replied, and he seemed genuine.

'And do you employ other female creators?'

He frowned and busied himself reading the menu. 'No.'.

A man sat at the bar a few metres from their table. It was getting darker now but Kitty knew that tall, lithe and *sexy* body. Pierre sat and adjusted his jacket, making himself comfortable on the high stool. Kitty swore she could smell his distinct scent but that would be impossible from this distance. She closed her eyes and concentrated, conjured up the scent. Perhaps she just knew it too well and imagined it?

Henri's knee knocked into hers under the table. It was impossible not to compare aromas. One was distinct, yet subtle, strong and all-man with its deep cedar and woody tones. The other, while also unique, was an in-your-face scent that took over and eliminated any other smell in the immediate vicinity. It was floral and...not as intoxicating.

Was one better than the other? Kitty had an opinion but... what did she know? And there seemed to be plenty of appetite and market for both.

Kitty pulled her gaze away from Pierre's back and focused on Henri. A waiter arrived to take their orders. She listened attentively to Henri tell an amusing story about a member of his staff. Kitty noticed it was about a female employee who'd done something silly at the party. Goosebumps skittered across her skin and she chided herself. She was being too sensitive. Henri was kind and sincere, he wasn't a chauvinist. She'd met many of those in her time, and he didn't fit the bill; she wouldn't waste her time in his company if that were the case. And his company was entertaining with his easy smile and polite conversation.

'Let's do something fun and go to Nice for the weekend,' he announced with enthusiasm. Kitty couldn't help but smile.

'That would be great! I've not been there yet, but the launch of Pierre's latest perfume is this Saturday.'

'We could miss it.' His grin was mischievous. Kitty thought he meant it.

'Pierre attended your event and he said that while you are competitors, everyone supports each other.'

He nodded thoughtfully. 'That is true.'. 'Speak of the devil.' He gestured towards the bar. 'The man himself.' Kitty glanced up and their eyes connected.

Pierre continued to sit alone, nursing a whisky tumbler. He wore a dark suit with his shirt collar undone and his hair was messy. Kitty controlled the hitch of her breath. He always had such an effect on her.

'How is the picking?' Henri asked breaking her out of her reverie.

'Good. I'm enjoying it. I love being surrounded by the scent of the roses. It has become one of my favourites.'

'Now that you've experienced where the raw source material comes from, you surely do not need to attend every day?'

'They are relying on me. I'd said I'd help...'

'Don't feel committed, he has a bunch of seasoned pickers he relies upon.'

Kitty nodded. Did Henri detect something in her pensive pause?

'You need to be careful of him.'

Kitty chuckled nervously. 'Why?'

'Other than being a notorious womaniser, Pierre killed his brother.'

Kitty sat up; her hand clutched to her chest. 'What do you mean?'

'It was when he was a teenager. He had a younger brother he was responsible for looking after. His parents were always busy, working or away—.'

'What about the nanny, Mrs Roubillard?'

Henri shrugged. 'I don't know. It was a road accident. Pierre was with a group of friends, and they were cycling outside of town. There are some steep hills and curves in the roads around the mountains.' Kitty nodded. Henri paused as their meals arrived. Henri commenced eating and spoke in between mouthfuls of food. Kitty held her breath as she waited.

'Report was that he was having too much fun with his friends and they rode ahead and left the brother behind.'

'What was the brother's name?' she asked.

'Louis.' He chewed some more, glancing at Pierre at the bar. 'Anyway, the brother was hit by a car. Pierre didn't know, he was riding so far ahead. They had to cycle back to find out, and by then, it was too late.'

'Where you part of the group of friends?'

'No, Pierre and I have never been close. We've always been acquaintances, nothing more.' Henri continued to eat his meal in silence. Kitty had lost her appetite.

In the encroaching dimness of the bar, Pierre cast a sad

shadow. Until a woman in an emerald frock sat on the stool next to him, her long black hair rippling down her back. She sipped her own drink and leaned one arm along the back of his barstool. He leaned in to hear what she said.

A sharp stab pierced her chest. She wanted to be the one receiving Pierre's attention, those gentle hands caressing her, those smouldering eyes focused in her direction. Damn it, she was jealous. With clarity she realised she'd done the one thing she didn't want to do: she'd fallen for the womanising, bad-boy millionaire.

Chapter Thirteen

The glistening blue pool reminded Kitty of home. She sat by the pool at the villa protected by a large outdoor umbrella. Nonetheless, the heat of the sun's rays penetrated the thin cloth of the shade and bore down upon her skin. The heat was so oppressive it was a relief to dive into the cool waters.

She loved the heat. Her housemates claimed it was purgatory, yet they sat in the sun with a thin application of sun cream. Kitty wore her wide-brimmed hat and long-sleeved rashie, which the others thought was hilarious.

In a rare moment of rest, Adrienne and Raph joined them, in between handing out drinks and snacks. Kitty lay her head back and relaxed. Just for a moment she was like any other tourist in the south of France.

A man appeared on the terrace carrying packages and Raph went over to accept delivery. 'What is it, honey?' Adrienne asked as he returned, his arms full of boxes.

'Delivery for Kitty!' he declared.

Kitty sat up and placed her feet to the ground while the others gathered around. 'I'm not expecting anything.' Raph placed the assortment at the end of her sunchair, which almost toppled with the weight.

'Open it up, and let's see,' Julia said as she sat next to her, searching for a note or card. 'Found it! Here, read this,' she screeched and thrust an envelope into Kitty's hand.

Kitty opened it to reveal a small black card. She read the words to herself.

'Hey, not fair. Tell us what it says!' demanded Sofia.

Dearest Kitty,

Please accept my thanks and gratitude for attending the launch of our latest perfume this evening for House of Joubert. With the help of Mrs Roubillard, I have chosen these items especially for you to wear. I hope I have chosen well and that you feel as beautiful in them as I know you will look. A car will collect you at 7 p.m. I look forward to seeing you there.

Pierre

'Girlfriend, what's going on? This is your second perfume party, and me and the gang are slaving away every day in the lab learning the trade, but you're getting the exclusive invites from the big houses? Something ain't right here...' Marianna stood in front of her with hands on hips.

'I've been helping at the harvest...'

'Girl, we know you're doing a lot more than picking flowers,' interjected Henrietta with a wicked grin.

'Adrienne and Raph,' Julia turned to them, 'who usually attends these events? Have you been before?'

'*Mai, oui*, yes, over the years, we've been to many. Perhaps when they were less extravagant. Now, they are large affairs. The staff of the perfume house attend, and people involved in the industry, many buyers and trade experts. Kitty has been working with both large perfume houses in Grasse, so that's why she's been extended an invitation. It is special and so exciting!' Adrienne threw her a look, and Kitty guessed it might be odd that she'd been invited. And even more strange that the owner of one of those houses was showering her with gifts.

Adrienne's speech satisfied the students, though.

Kitty lifted the lid off the largest square box. Tissue paper hid the contents, and she removed the layers before lifting out a light-as-a-feather chiffon dress. When she held it up, the skirt billowed in various shades of pink – pale, deep maroon and lollypop. A piece of fabric draped over one shoulder which would leave the other bare. The girls in the group let out an audible gasp, and Marianna reached for the tag.

'It's Dolce & Gabbana! Oh my God!' They touched the fine cloth with reverence. It was the sheerest Kitty had ever seen.

'It is divine! You will look like a goddess in that dress,' Adrienne said.

She next opened a rectangular-shaped shoe box. Inside sat a cream pair of strappy stiletto heels matching the shades of the dress. Little gems sparkled along the edges. In another smaller package was a matching clutch in the same colour and design with gemstones along the handle.

Only left now was a collection of smaller boxes. Kitty's mouth went dry as she gazed at the faces of those around her displaying awe, the girls green with envy. They danced on their toes in impatience for her to reveal the contents.

Kitty felt like Cinderella heading to the ball.

Kitty lifted out a purple silk pouch adorning the words *Blanco Fine Jewels*. Marianna squealed. '*Blanco Fine Jewels* is the finest Spanish jewellery company. Their jewels are exquisite,' she whispered as she drew her hands up to cover her mouth.

Holding her breath, Kitty lifted out a rose gold chain. At its apex, a closed circle pendant sparkled with lines of circular gems. Were they diamonds? Surely not.

Marianna examined it. 'Those are tiny pave-set diamonds. Please tell me you have the matching set?'

The next box was heavier. Kitty flicked off the lid to reveal a solid gold bangle with more gems. She'd never worn diamonds before. The bangle sparkled in the sunlight as she slipped it onto her arm. The girls jumped up and down.

'Open the third please, let's see.'

It contained matching rose gold hoop earrings with another scattering of diamonds.

Chad pushed to the front of the group, shoving the girls out of his way. 'This guy is seriously smokin' for you, Kitty. This is some expensive shit, and he's pulling out all stops. Either that, or he's so rich, it doesn't matter.' With his piece said, Chad dived into the pool, making a splash on the paved terrace.

'I guess I don't have to loan you a dress this evening,' Adrienne joked.

'Can we help you get dressed again?' Sofia asked and Julia joined in. It wasn't lost on Kitty that this time they didn't demand, they asked her.

The door of the Bentley clicked shut and the chauffer assisted Kitty out of the car and ensured her designer dress was clear of the vehicle.

Wow. Wow. Wow.

This place was incredible. The staircase in front of her wasn't sweeping and tall this time, but it was in no way less grand. The circular drive leading to the building was congested with fancy European cars; in the middle was an opulent fountain with waves of flowing water and at its base lay a garden bed with flowers in full bloom.

The location of tonight's launch was the Monte Carlo casino. It was a majestic, old building standing sentry over Monaco. The road from Grasse hugged the mountain edge on one side and the dazzling Mediterranean on the other. Kitty had blinked as she'd entered another country. Her mind was blown! She'd left France behind with nothing but a simple trip across an invisible border.

Inside, she stood before an open, impressive yellow-beige door towering above her. Kitty blew out a breath; once again she felt like Cinderella, this time entering the ball, alone, nervous and unsure of what lay ahead. She had the ensemble: dress, shoes, jewellery and the girls had once again made her beautiful. Not for the first time, she twisted the necklace between her fingers, enjoying the smoothness of the circular pendant and the tiny bumps of the jewels. She tried not to think of its value.

Okay, she could do this. Taking a few slow steps forward, she lifted her gaze to the ornate and painted ceiling with its gold trimmings. Enormous chandeliers cast a glow around the room so that it appeared draped in gilt. It was an ostentatious space. The room didn't smell of money, it screamed luxury. Adding to the effect were hundreds of guests; men in tuxedos and women dressed in designer gowns and dripping in jewellery. Excited chatter filled the space. A symphony orchestra played background music so divine and soft it could have floated her away. She took another step forward, and the crowd parted.

Kitty twirled on the spot to allow the important guest behind her, to pass. There was no one there. Self-conscious, she inched forward while people stared. She put on her most regal smile and walked with fake confidence, willing her feet not to trip in the high heels.

And there he was. Like an apparition, Pierre appeared.

Oh, la. Dressed in formal wear, his unruly curls tamed. He didn't smile, but Kitty felt his magnetic pull. His look was one filled with longing. She could feel his heat, taste his desire. Her heart lurched at the thought that tonight she might be here for Pierre.

Little hands tugged on his arms and he turned away, smiling at the children who surrounded him, each resplendent in pretty dresses or pant suits. Kitty's stomach did a funny little dip at the sight of Claude in trousers and a shirt with a tie. The kids shouted at Pierre, vying for his attention. With a last swift glance, but one she thought was filled with meaning, Pierre held up an object, and they stood in rapture as he appeared to explain something. The children stood silent, the ever-present force of Ms Dubois at the rear.

A figure dropped in front of her, and Kitty squealed. A circus performer dangled precariously on a round ring attached to a coloured curtain falling from the ceiling. Her supple legs twirled into shapes that made Kitty go cross-eyed. The woman coiled towards another on the ground with sticks that she spun into the air at high speed and thankfully caught. Kitty noticed a trapeze hung from the ceiling with acrobats flying through the air.

Pierre and his company had spared no expense to deliver a signature event.

A waiter offered her a flute of champagne that she accepted gratefully as she focused on the acrobatics. She drank the delicious fizzy liquid as she tried to work out what to do after the circus show finished.

The perfume! Of course. She must check it out. Captivated by the room and the people—or Pierre— Kitty hadn't noticed the new scent. Even her senses were rendered void at the sight her eyes were feasting upon.

Now, she couldn't focus on anything else. A life-sized gold perfume bottle with the trademark pink lid stood in one corner. A tap released liquid that gushed into an intricate piping system that circled the bottle and landed in what appeared to be a crystal pool. More wow factor! Even watching the liquid swirl to the base, she couldn't believe it was perfume. It couldn't be. The cost would be astronomical.

Kitty looked left and right and convinced no one watched, stretched her finger out to touch the flow. Her finger was close when a body appeared beside her, a gorgeous woman wearing red. Her lips were full and luscious, and large, dangly diamond earrings hung from her ears.

'Here.' She offered a slim white tester of the perfume. 'It's called *Jardin d'Amour.*' The words released like a purr.

Kitty translated. 'Garden of Love.'

'*Oui*, yes.' The woman confirmed and told her the story of the perfume.

Kitty closed her eyes, held the card to her nose and let the scent envelope her. She picked out the elements. 'Musk, vanilla, bergamot and maybe lemon?'

The perfume transported her to a party like this one. There was fun, frivolity and its own uniqueness. There were light and bubbly drinks that tickled your nose. Gaiety would be the word to sum up her feelings.

A hand touched her arm, and she was caught unawares. Her champagne spilled as she jerked. Henri kissed her forehead in greeting and she smiled warmly in return, happy to see a familiar face.

The representative of the *House of Joubert* offered her a bag. 'This is for you, mademoiselle, a gift for attending this evening.'

'*Merci*,' Kitty replied and snuck a look inside the gold drawstring bag. There was a 100-millilitre bottle of *Jardin d'Amour*. Kitty scanned the room, and every person present had a bag. Her brain worked out the math. That was a lot of concentrated perfume to be giving away. *Ching. Ching.*

'You look *absolutement* stunning,' Henri crooned in her ear. The warmth of his hand upon her waist penetrated through the sheer fabric of her dress.

Chapter Fourteen

enri's eyes devoured her and there was no mistaking the admiration that pooled within them. His hand lingered at her waist. With a deep sense of what felt like nostalgia, she wanted to enjoy the sensation of his hand against her, wanted to long for him and the responsible person he was.

In his three-piece grey suit with baby pink tie, Henri not only looked ravishing, his colour palette matched her dress. He was all Clark Kent look-alike tonight with his black-rimmed glasses and slick hair and chiselled jaw. Was he like the super-hero? Calm and staid underneath his good looks? There was no mistaking he was a very attractive man, and had many admirable qualities, unfortunately he wasn't the one that stole her breath away.

Kitty glanced across the crowded ballroom to the man she wanted to be standing with. A sea of media personnel surrounded Pierre and were kept enraptured with whatever he was saying.

Henri murmured close to her ear. 'You're so beautiful, Kitty.' The whisper of the words tickled her ear and made her shiver but not for the reasons he wanted. 'Are all Australian girls as pretty as you?' She shrugged with a smile. 'It's wonderful you're here tonight. I was too busy at my event celebrating the success of our perfume. Did you love it?'

The party or the perfume? Neither had been amazing. Kitty pulled back and watched his features change as the seconds passed, a flicker of uncertainty appearing.

'Tell me about it, Henri. 'Did you create the *Lys Blancs* perfume?'

'I was integral to its creation, but like all our perfumes, it is first created by some of our expert staff. I'm sure you met them.' She was sure she hadn't met any of the lab staff, but she nodded anyway. He commenced a lengthy dialogue about the concept and elements and his contribution.

'It's quite musky,' she offered.

Henri appeared thrilled and agreed. 'Plus, the chemical component reacts well together creating—'

'You wear the cologne tonight,' she interrupted.

Henri leaned in close, his breath against her cheek. 'I do. You are very perceptive. I knew from the first day we met that you were good with fragrance.'

'Did you? That's very kind. I think my skills have improved immensely since then. My dream is to become a creator of beautiful perfume.' Kitty sighed.

'My family adore you,' he continued as if she hadn't revealed her most vulnerable self.

'Really?' She was surprised.

'Oh, yes, my grandmother particularly.' Kitty found that hard to believe. 'She approves.' *Hmm?* His eyes now smouldered in her direction, and he pivoted his hips against her. 'Yes,' he whispered, 'and she never likes anyone.' Gently, he tugged her closer until their bodies were touching and he bowed his head towards hers, his lips parting. A slight panic fluttered in her chest. He was going to kiss her? No...But then he belched and she reared backwards.

'Oh, my apologies.' His face blanched, and droplets of sweat appeared on his brow.

'Henri? Are you okay?'

'I'm not feeling well.' He reached for his handkerchief to wipe his brow with rough strokes. 'You have to be so careful at these places. Germs are everywhere,' he said and kept mopping his forehead before covering his mouth. 'Can you please excuse me, Kitty?' He rushed away.

Pierre found Kitty standing alone at the bar. He slowed his steps, wanting to observe her without notice. His body came alive just at the sight of her. She wore the dress as though it had been made specially for her; the jewels sparkled at her throat and wrist, and her usually wavy hair was secured neatly into an elaborate roll. He preferred it loose and tumbling over her shoulders. But he appreciated her one bare shoulder, pale and creamy in the light. His fingers itched to caress that arm, to cause her to gasp and erupt in shivers.

'It's a crime that such a beautiful woman is standing alone at a party.' The smile she offered him was sweet, alluring and yet downright sexy. He noticed her scent immediately. 'You're wearing my perfume,' he said.

'Yes, I adore it. It's exquisite.' He glowed in her praise. 'Do I detect lemon as a top note?'

Pierre threw his head back and laughed. Only Kitty could cause him to guffaw so unrestrainedly. 'You're smart. I don't ever want to hear you say that you're a joke. It's not true. You are talented.'

Her lips parted in surprise and he had to hold himself rigid to prevent crushing his mouth against hers.

'It's true,'

'Do you really think so?'

'Yes.'

'Will you continue to teach me?' He nodded; he wanted to teach her many things. An arm slid across his shoulders and he turned. It was one of his models, dressed to suit the fragrance and a living, breathing advertisement. She was stunning, they all were, and he was grateful for their hard work, but tonight, he had eyes only for Kitty. He thanked the model, kissed her on both cheeks and sent her away.

'Are the rumours true?' she asked him.

'What rumours?

'That you sleep with different women every night yet never commit? That you never leave a party alone?' Her gaze was strong and her words strident and challenging.

'Do I look like the life of this party?'

She squared her shoulders. 'Yes, you're the boss, owner, creator, it's about you. Women are lining up to get their paws all over you—'

'Paws?'

He laughed as she demonstrated with her hands on his arms.

Kitty turned serious. 'Do you have a girlfriend?' He shook his head. 'A wife?' He cracked a smile and shook again. She didn't return his smile. 'When was the last time you were in a relationship?'

Surreptitiously, another elegant woman sidled up to him, this time, older and sophisticated, dripping in colourful jewels. Her glare was steely but Kitty detected a hint of sadness at their corners. She stood with a distinguished gentleman wearing steel-framed glasses, his fine silver hair balding in places; together they made a formidable pair.

'Hello, darling.' Her words were formal and stiff and there was no traditional French kiss.

'Hello, Mother, Father. May I introduce Mademoiselle Kitty Landers.'

Kitty offered her hand in greeting. Pierre's mother scanned Kitty from top to toe with derision and ignored the introduction.

'The children shouldn't be at such an extravagant party. Children and luxury perfume do not mix.'

'They're not harming anyone, Mother.'

'Your time is better suited focusing on more important matters.'

Pierre gritted his teeth. He would not respond to these age-old criticisms. He noticed the flash of disdain in Kitty's direction, the intent clear. If he stood with a daughter of the Monaco Royal family, or one of the many local millionairesses, or even a woman from a notable upper-class family, his mother wouldn't be so disrespectful.

A distinguished politician addressed his parents, and they

moved away. Pierre signalled to the barman for a bottle off the top shelf and his other hand reached for Kitty. 'Let's get out of here.' As she gazed up at him with certainty and self-assuredness, a wave of protectiveness pulsed through him.

Kitty didn't hesitate. She followed him, matching his strides across the spacious room. People stopped him to express their congratulations, and women offered sultry smiles. His pace didn't falter as he continued through the foyer and down the short set of stairs. Caught by surprise, the valet jumped to attention.

'Throw me the keys, I'll collect the car.' The keys flew through the air, and Pierre caught them in one low swoop.

'Hop in.' Pierre opened the door to a bright red Ferrari.

Kitty hesitated. She was a smart girl. Would she resist?

She stared into his eyes, assessing him. Her lips lifted at the corners. She should resist but she didn't. Kitty grasped the hem of her dress to protect it as she slid into in the low leather seat.

He turned the ignition, and the engine rumbled to life. Next to him, Kitty's dress parted, leaving one leg bare to the thigh.

Oh, boy.

'Do you like the dress and jewels?'

'Pierre, oh my gosh, it's all so beautiful.' She caressed the fabric. He'd like to be under that hand. 'And the jewellery! It's the finest I've ever worn. Thank you so much for loaning it to me. The girls at the villa said this is a Spanish brand and super exclusive.'

'Yes, the best. But it is yours to keep.'

'Are they diamonds?'

'Yes.'

'It's stunning,' she whispered, and continued. 'It's too much and too expensive. I can't accept it.'

Pierre changed gears with force, and the car propelled forward, lurching them both back into their seats. They left the lights of the Monaco harbour behind them.

'I'm glad you love it. You look stunning and deserve nice things. It's a gift, I'm not accepting it back.'

'You don't even know me.'

Kitty kept on about how she could not accept such an outrageous gift. 'No, that's enough. I want to give you these things.'

'Thank you.' Her words were barely audible but he was happy she dropped her refusal.

Adrenalin raced through his veins; he felt agitated and reckless, and he drove too fast, the kilometres ticking over. Lost in another sphere, he let the world race by. The roads curved, and he moved as one with the vehicle, deftly avoiding cars approaching in the opposite direction. He knew these roads, had driven them his entire life and had no fear. Until he heard Kitty gasp and grip the handle of the door as a truck approached in the opposite direction. He slowed and crawled the car into the nearest pull-over lane at the crest of a high curve. He released the window to let in fresh, cool, night air and raked it into his lungs. He slowed his breathing and cut the engine.

The world around them was black. The dark and ominous ocean sat in front, soft white peaks occasionally appearing. The Principality of Monaco was well behind them.

'I'm sorry. I forgot myself for a moment.' Without looking at her, he reached for the bottle in the rear seat and unscrewed the lid before taking a long swig. He offered it to her and she did the same. He was impressed.

'Nice car,' she said.

It had the perfect effect, and his laughter erupted for the second time that evening.

'I didn't mean to frighten you.'

'I wasn't frightened.' He turned in his seat and raised one eyebrow.

'Okay, maybe a little. Why the hell were you driving like that?'

He didn't answer. 'It was like the devil himself was chasing you,' Kitty said.

'Do you believe in God?'

'Random question. Um, no, not really. Do you?'

'No.' Followed by more nips of whisky.

'Slow down cowboy.' She snatched the bottle from his grip.

Pierre clenched and uncurled his fingers a few times. The spirit was doing its trick, his body loosened, and the coils in his stomach unknotted.

'You shouldn't believe everything you hear.'

She shrugged. 'Okay, I won't, but I do see with my own eyes.'

'What do you see now?'

'I see a man in pain running from something, not being entirely honest. But also, a very attractive, kind, and caring man.'

It was hard to hear compliments. Even harder to believe them. He was used to living up to his reputation. Of being the bad boy, drinking and partying all night, accepting the advances of attractive and attentive women. Being who they all wanted him to be. But Pierre Joubert was only one thing; a man who had killed his brother.

'Today is the anniversary of my brother's death.' He snatched the bottle back. 'My parents pretend it never happened. As if I never had a brother, as if they didn't have two sons. And what's more, they planned our perfume launch for the same day. Is that callous?'

He dare not look at her. What would he see in her eyes? Pity? Sadness? Sympathy? He didn't want any of those feelings directed towards him. He stared out the windscreen, taking in the black, dark ocean.

'People cope in different ways. I imagine the last thing parents want to do is celebrate on the day their son died. But perhaps they needed distraction?'

He turned to consider her then and found clear aqua eyes boring into him.

'Oh, yes, they're good at distraction. Sending me away to boarding school after my brother died. That distraction worked well for them. Out of sight, out of mind.'

'How old were you?'

'Twelve.' His voice broke, and he disguised it by taking another swig from the bottle.

Kitty placed her hand on his thigh. 'How old was your brother?'

'Nine.'

'I'm so sorry. That must have been dreadful and incredibly hard for all of you.'

Pierre shook his head. 'You'd think I'd be over it by now, it's almost thirty years ago, for fuck's sake.' He slammed his fist against the steering wheel. 'My parents have never forgiven me.

Will never forgive me. I was supposed to be looking after him that day. It was the weekend and I was cycling with my mates. My parents were working; they were always working. Because they were busy, they insisted my brother tag along everywhere with me. Louis was small and slow. My friends ignored him and I did, too. He rode along at the back of the group until suddenly, he wasn't there anymore. I remember being annoyed but trailed back to find him, but it was too late. He'd been hit by a car, on these roads, not far from here, and was killed instantly.'

'It's not your fault. I'm sure your parents don't blame you.'

Pierre snorted and drank again. 'Trust me, they do. They sent me away. The sight of me repulsed them. I've never been good enough since. Even at a young age, it was Louis who had the natural flair for perfume making, was a born *nez*. Then he was gone. As the only son, I had to fill the gap. The business has never run to their satisfaction, profits never high enough, products not the best, competitors too close.'

Shame washed over Pierre. It was this Australian girl; she'd given him a loose tongue. He never talked this much even with whisky in his belly. And he never talked about his brother, ever. He needed to maintain control. Gulping more of the spirit, he gunned the engine to life.

'No!' She flung her arm across his chest. 'You can't drive, you've had too much to drink.' Her face drained of colour.

'Don't be silly,' he slurred. 'I've driven these roads a thousand times. I'm perfectly capable.'

'Besides,' he added, 'this car almost drives itself.' He blinked once, then twice, but he had to admit that his vision had blurred. He placed pressure against the accelerator again.

'No, please, Pierre. Don't.' He looked at her, this beautiful girl who had somehow charmed him and made him talk. But what he saw now was fear. She was frightened and shaking and clutched his arm in restraint. If it had been only him in the car, of course he would have driven, he would have driven too fast, dangerously, deliberately dicing with death, not frightened of the consequences. But he wasn't alone. Kitty was with him.

'Can you drive a Ferrari?'

She sank back into her seat and lifted her arm. 'Well, there's a first time for everything.'

They swapped seats; Pierre hated being in the passenger side of his luxury car. Kitty turned the car over. 'It's meant to be driven with power and confidence,' he said to her as she examined the knobs and buttons on the dash.

'Are you worried I might crash?'

'No.' He wasn't. Positioned behind the wheel, the split in her dress was more prominent and with her feet on the pedals, her legs were tantalisingly revealed. She didn't notice, but that was the kind of girl Kitty was. Any other woman would have deliberately parted the split in her dress. Not Kitty, and that made it the most seductive ever.

He placed his hand on her bare leg and caressed the smooth skin. She glanced down at his hand and let seconds pass before putting it back in his lap. 'I must concentrate,' she said.

A long while after, they pulled into his drive. 'That is the slowest this car has ever been driven and the longest it has ever taken me to return from Monaco,' he said with a smile.

'Well, you should be thanking me for delivering you home safely.' She pouted.

'Thank you, Kitty.' The words hung in the air.

He opened his passenger door and tumbled onto the

pebbled drive, landing on his hands and knees. An outside light illuminated, and a door opened.

'Oh, Mrs Roubillard,' Kitty spoke. 'Thank goodness. Pierre, um, he's had too much to drink.' From his position on the ground, Pierre imagined the wordless exchange between the pair. He tried to lift to his feet but his balance was off and he fell sideways.

Laying on the ground, an apparition appeared before him. Kitty resplendent in soft chiffon pink, her pale skin illuminated in the moonlight, her blonde hair, angelic. Man, she was perfect. Innocent. Feminine. Too good for him.

Next to her stood Mrs Roubillard wearing a long, white muslin night gown, her silver hair twirled haphazardly upon her head, wisps standing out in the light. As a child, he'd thought her night attire the funniest thing. Now, it was a sight for sore eyes. Someone cared for him, any time of day or night regardless of how he behaved.

'Thank you, love, for bringing him home. You lift under one side, and I'll do the other. At least we can help each other.'

Pierre tuned out. They were treating him like a baby, and he didn't want to listen. He was a grown man who could look after himself. Hands found his armpits, and, uncomfortable with their help, he shucked out of their grip. Mrs Roubillard tsked like he was a naughty child. They tried again, and he was soon on his feet and directed to the house. Inside, at the staircase leading to the upper level, he flicked their hands away and ascended, holding tight to the railing.

'I'll get him settled, Kitty and then I'll make us both a hot cocoa and I'll show you to the spare room. It's late and there's picking in the morning.'

Chapter Fifteen

Kitty whipped off her picking apron, washed up at the taps in the shed and headed straight for the lab. During the hours of picking, alone with her thoughts, she'd come up with an idea for not one perfume, but a series. All linked, all related and her original idea. She was busting to get started.

In the early hours of the morning, she'd wasted time peeking over her shoulder and waiting for Pierre to appear. Unable to sleep after last night, she'd tossed and turned and today, all she wanted was to see him; check he was okay and offer comfort. Her heart weighed heavy at his revelation.

But he'd never shown. Where was he? Sleeping off his hangover? In the short time she'd known him, he'd never shirked his responsibilities. The fields had been extra quiet without his presence.

Prepped and ready to go in the lab, she hesitated. Were her ideas good enough? Would it work? Peering behind her again, she wished she could conjure up Pierre to chat with him about her idea and ask what he thought. Damn, sick of prevaricating, she decided to get on with it. Kitty rearranged the vials, glass jars, and other equipment one last time. There was no harm in practising.

Hours passed and she'd tried numerous variations, different elements and mixtures and none were right. Kitty threw another dash of liquid down the sink, rolling her shoulders, she tried to release the tension. Maybe she was a joke? It was hard to keep those voices at bay. Fatigue washed over her from her late night.

'You skipped lunch?' Mrs Roubillard said as she entered carrying food.

Kitty jumped. 'Oh, Mrs Roubillard, you scared me.' Noticing the plate laden with food, she apologised. 'You don't need to look after me.'

'I enjoy it.' The housekeeper smiled and placed the plate on the sideboard. 'Plus, you need to eat.'

'I haven't seen Pierre today. Is he okay?'

The housekeeper paused, as if weighing up her words. 'He's all right. I served him coffee and croissants this morning, which he ate before rushing into the office. I'm sure he's also avoiding you.'

'Hiding?' Kitty scrunched her face up in confusion.

'*Oui*,' Mrs Roubillard said, her smile sly. 'I know him well. He aches terribly for the loss of his brother but no one would ever know. I don't know how you did it, my love, but he broke down in front of you, and he'll be shy about that now.'

'He told you?'

'He mumbled a few things, but it wasn't hard to work out. I was worried about him earlier in the evening, given it was the anniversary of the death, so it was no surprise he turned up like that.' She touched Kitty on the arm, 'He was fortunate to have you. I fear one day he'll not be so lucky.'

'You don't think his brother's death is his fault, do you?'

'No! He was a child. It was an accident. But despite me telling him that a million times over, he takes it to heart. I don't think he'd have taken it as hard if his parents had reacted differently.' Mrs Roubillard wiped her hands down her apron and cast her gaze around the room, looking uncomfortable as if she'd said too much. 'A café to go with your lunch?'

Kitty nodded in agreement. 'Mrs Roubillard?' She called out as the woman went to leave. 'Thank you for the clothes and jewellery for the launch. Pierre said you helped him pick them out. They were divine.'

The woman shook her head. 'It was him, *ma cherie*.'

Kitty picked at the food on the plate while thinking. An idea struck her that might save her project. With renewed vigour, she tried again. 'One more shot today and then I'll have a break.' She checked her watch. 'Shoot!' she double-checked the time on her phone. She'd missed class. Henri would not be happy. At some point, Mrs Roubillard returned with her hot drink, but Kitty didn't even notice, and the coffee turned cold.

Kitty inhaled one more time, checking the elements and the notes, the combinations, the effect on her. It had worked, had come out like she'd imagined and transported her just as she'd hoped. Satisfied, she closed her eyes and let the fatigue wash over her.

Placing the labelled vial in the far corner of one shelf, she vowed to add to that collection. Would Pierre like it? Still think she had talent? Heading out of the sheds, she glanced around her again, wishing one last time to see him. A plan had been brewing in her head, and she was keen to speak with him. Plus, she wanted to see him, be with him...

The trip into town was short on the bicycle. Up ahead, she saw Henri coming out of the grocer, and she hurried.

'Henri!' she yelled to catch his attention.

A smile appeared on his face but it seemed forced and there was no delight in his usually expressive eyes. 'You missed class again.' For the first time, he didn't kiss her hand in greeting. He shuffled the bags of produce he held from hand to hand.

'I'm sorry. I was working on an idea...'

'At Pierre's lab?' He grimaced as if the words were distasteful.

Kitty paused at his reaction but she was too excited not to share. '*Oui*. Can I tell you about it? Over a drink? You can tell me what you think.'

Henri was amazing at the chemical side to producing perfume, he'd know if the elements worked. In one swift movement, the clouds hid the sun and the world around them dimmed, matching his expression.

'Hallo, Kitty.' His sister appeared beside him also laden with bags.

'Let's do that after class tomorrow.' Henri moved away.

'We've got to run,' his sister said, holding up their bags, 'it's *Maman's* birthday and we are making dinner, *au revoir!*'

As she watched them leave, a child ran into her legs, tumbling onto the ground near her feet. She curled up into a ball and two larger, older boys stopped nearby, their chests heaving, rocks in their hands. They shouted at the child in sharp French, their faces giving away that they were not dishing out compliments.

'Hey,' she addressed them and they dropped their weapons before pulling a face at the child and racing away. Kitty threw the bike on its side and kneeled down to the child. The girl was sweating and hot to touch and had grazed her knees. Silent tears streamed down her cheeks creating dirty trails.

'Let me help you.' She gripped the child by the arms and raised her to her feet. There was a bench nearby and she moved them towards it to sit. 'Ouch, that looks sore.' Kitty examined her two bleeding knees. 'We'll have to get you cleaned up.'

The girl stared, her little cherub mouth wide open and her eyes transfixed on Kitty. Kitty laughed and the girl responded in like, forgetting about the boys chasing her with rocks and the scrapes on her knees. The girl leaned against Kitty's shoulder, crooked her head and whispered, 'Papa Pierre.'

'Do you mean my perfume?' Kitty smiled. 'Yes. I'm wearing his new perfume. Gosh, aren't you smart? But does that mean, do you . . . do you live at *Maison de Roses*?'

'*Maison de Roses*! *Oui, Maison de Roses.*'

'Can you show me the way?' She gestured with her fingers in a walking motion. 'We need to get you home and cleaned up.' With one hand guiding her bike, and the other in the small grip of the girl, they walked away.

'Goal!' shrieked Claude, holding his arms up in victory.

Pierre geed up his opposing team as the children pouted and dragged their feet in the spacious back garden. '*Allez les enfants,*' he encouraged as they huddled together talking tactics.

'Keep going!' he shouted as Ms Dubois brought out plates

of afternoon tea, and he abandoned the game to assist. Fruit and vegetables encompassing the colours of the rainbow were displayed on the outdoor table. He insisted on a healthy environment and the development of good habits at Rose House. Sometimes he grimaced; what he produced here was probably more idyllic than most family homes. He often worried he was setting them up for failure should they, when they, were adopted. In fact, he knew what he was doing; he was creating the childhood he'd yearned for. Hearing the screams of joy and commiserations from the backyard game of football, he shook those thoughts away. Until these children were housed and living somewhere else, he'd provide utopia for them. It was the least they deserved.

With his commitments at the factory completed for the day, he'd chosen to spend the afternoon at Rose House. School lessons were finished and it was time for a snack. The heat of the summer day had disappeared, the gardens surrounding the house were cool in the shade and the children needed to work off steam before dinner and evening routine.

Jude entered the backyard holding Kitty's hand. Pierre did a double take and pretended that Kitty didn't make his entire body come alive. Inwardly, he shrivelled thinking of last night, of his drunken stupor and worse, loose tongue. Jude's lips down-turned and her head bowed. He rushed over, kneeling to her level on the backstairs. He tickled her ribs and within moments, the girl was giggling.

'Thank you for bringing her home,' he said to Kitty after hearing what had happened.

She smiled and he lit up on the inside. 'You're welcome. Her knees are banged up.'

'Yes.' He addressed Jude. 'These wounds will need a band-aid, I think. Let's go.' He offered his hand, which she took willingly.

'You'll do it?' Kitty sounded unsure. 'I can...'

'No, it's fine. I'll fix her up.'

Pierre heard the squeals as he descended the long and winding staircase well before he reached the back garden. Jude raced away from him and joined in the fun. The children were in a pyramid, with Kitty at the base, some of the older boys, and the lighter children on top, kneeling to form the shape. As he arrived, the children fell into a heap onto the grass, laughing—Kitty, too. Pierre smiled at the scene in front of him.

He was about to join in when Melodie whispered in his ear. His gut twisted. Nodding his thanks, he turned to welcome the inspector. Inspections were regular and normal.

'*Bonjour monsieur*.' The man's nod was curt. The inspector from the government department was a civil servant employed to check that they were complying with the various regulations and rules imposed upon them. Pierre hadn't seen this fellow before and his abrupt greeting had apprehension bubbling to the surface. Pierre reached to loosen his collar but realised he wasn't wearing a tie. Instead, he put on his professional demeanour, very different to how he'd been acting with the children this afternoon.

Pierre had been gone for ages. Kitty was breathless at the endless games and suggested the children take a break and eat some fruit.

'You don't have to play with them, you know.' Melodie said as she handed her a cool drink.

Kitty sipped recalling that Pierre was playing with them when she'd arrived, a fact she confirmed with Melodie. '*Oui*, but he's a big kid. And every time he's here he does everything to ensure their life is perfect: the playing, the food. But life is not perfect, no?'

Pierre entered, flanked by an official-looking man carrying a briefcase, a clipboard and a pen. 'Who's that?' Kitty asked.

'Inspector. As a regulated children's home there are laws we must comply with. We are regularly inspected to ensure cleanliness, conditions and food regulations are being adhered to, etcetera.' She shrugged feigning nonchalance. Another member of staff entered the back garden, and Melodie waved. 'It's my night off!'

Kitty watched the inspector stop, turn, count on his fingers and write something down. Pierre frowned but his face cleared the moment Claude raced to his side to seek a high-five and ask something.

Kitty's breath caught. It could have been a scene between a father and his son. The depth of care expressed in Pierre's eyes could not be faked. He bent his head low, maintained eye contact and listened as if there wasn't an inspection being carried out right that minute. After Claude finished, Pierre replied and the boy listened with the same rapt attention. The affection between the pair was obvious.

And all of a sudden, as if a cloudy sky became clear and the dazzling sun had been released from hiding, it became obvious to Kitty. She took in her surroundings: the home, the children. Claude was ten, one of the children who had been at the home the longest. Kitty knew he had not been adopted, and there was a real risk that he wouldn't be. Younger children were desired, not the older youth, nearing puberty and the turbulent teenage years ahead.

Claude was a similar age to Louis when he died. But that wasn't why Pierre cared for him, she was sure. He cared for every child. Watching him now, it was so obvious she couldn't believe she hadn't realised before. He was making amends. Making up for his mistake. Giving life to others when he couldn't save his brother. She recalled his mother's remark at the launch. She had commented that Pierre should focus on important issues and not the children. He wasn't getting the approval he so sought from his parents, but he was seeking redemption in other ways. This was deeply personal.

Her eyes welled up for him, for the pain he carried. What would it take for Pierre to forgive himself?

The inspector spoke to Claude now, and Pierre's look became frosty. At the inspector's words, the boy clutched onto Pierre. Bad news? Kitty couldn't tell. The boy became inconsolable and Pierre latched onto him and spoke over his head to the inspector. The words seemed to brush over the older man without taking traction, his head shaking while his lips moved. He was counting again, Kitty realised. And then his gaze seemed to focus on each individual child before he spoke to Pierre whose gaze scanned the yard, too. The inspector rifled through his briefcase and extracted a folder. Inside he ripped out pages of paper and shoved it at Pierre.

Kitty observed the scene of the children playing. It was like she looked upon something different to the inspector. All she saw was fun, happiness and serenity. It was a small group of twenty or so that filled the enclosed back garden. A high wall secured around them with crawling vines over the Tuscan-rendered brick wall. Garden beds sat flush to the fence. The group was a mixture of boys and girls with happy faces, sweaty from play. It was obvious Claude was the eldest, most were four or five years old. Some, perhaps seven. Kitty inspected them closer and observed they were all well-dressed and clean. They didn't wear shoes, but the grass was soft under their feet. These orphaned children were well looked after and happy. Indignation pulsed through her and sat heavy in her chest at what the inspector might be insinuating. But she wouldn't speculate. Anyone watching these happy children would know they were well cared for.

With raised voices, it was clear Pierre disagreed and waved the papers about, shaking his head. The inspector left and Pierre embraced Claude.

'What is it, Pierre?'

It took a moment to find his words. '*Maison de Roses* is registered as a home for twenty children. At the moment we have twenty-one. The inspector said we must reduce our numbers back to twenty to comply with the regulations. He suggested that as there are other homes for older children, that Claude should be relocated as he is the eldest.'

Chapter Sixteen

Kitty strode ahead. She knew Henri would show interest in her creation.

Henri Beaumont leaned his back against the guesthouse, one leg cocked behind him and resting on the wall. It was the most relaxed she'd seen him. Peter, Chad and the others surrounded him.

Moving closer, it became obvious he was holding court, front and centre of the group, dominating the conversation. Her fellow students leaned in, listened, drinking in every word.

The bicycle wheels crunched on the pebble path, and he detected her approach. He offered his irresistible boyish grin and her shoulders sagged with relief.

Right now, she needed a friend. Her emotions were in a spin as she tried to make sense of the scene at the home and the anguish of both Pierre and Claude. Walking away left her with a combination of worry and uncertainty about Claude's future but also an unwavering belief that Pierre would fix it. Still, the circumstances sucked, and the mood at the home when she left was sombre.

'...in order to compete in a very crowded market, I have worked out that we can import tonnes of fresh flowers direct from India and Tunisia while still supporting a local economy. It makes business sense, and means we can produce a greater volume of fragrances each year and keep up with demand. If our company relied solely on local farmers, we wouldn't be in that position.'

Kitty cocked her head; she must have misheard. Beaumont de Villiers didn't use flowers from Grasse to make their perfume? The idea was preposterous given the region thrived upon the flower harvest and was something they were famous for.

'Here she is,' he said as she arrived beside him, and he kissed her hand.

'Is that a long-term solution, or will you try and increase your local flower presence in the future? Because as I understand it, most perfume houses have contracts direct with farmers for exclusive rights to their harvest.' Julia was smart and Kitty silently high-fived her.

Kitty counted her breaths in and out. One, two, three...

'Yes, but that has created the problem. There are so few farms left that are not contracted that if you do not have that relationship, you have no flowers.'

Nine, ten. 'You can't be serious Henri,' she interjected. 'You import flowers without using the local resources of your community?'

His foot landed to the earth, his stance tall and stiff but he softened it with a tight-lipped smile. 'You know nothing, Kitty, of the economics and business of producing perfume. It is not as simple as crooning over smells and spending days in labs producing a scent. Tonnes of flowers are required to produce one fragrance. How can we do that if there aren't enough flowers?' His tone was businesslike. Kitty sensed she was in dangerous territory and that he wouldn't like being shown up in front of the group.

'Plant more flowers?' Marianna laughed and the group joined her. With production only on their mind, they didn't care where the raw materials came from, like Henri. He was off the hook. They shook his hand, thanked him for the chat and wandered away.

Kitty knew her fellow guests studied at the most prestigious perfume school in Grasse, but they had little contact with the perfume houses. They were locked away in their labs, perfecting their formulas and chemical reactions, while she had been at the coalface picking those precious flowers. The blooms were the most important part of the process. The flowers needed to be perfect, tendered and cared for; that was how to produce the best perfume. Henri might be the head of the oldest house in Grasse and know the research and the economics of running a business, but he missed the romantic element of the process. He missed the nose aspect. He'd never admit it, but she suspected he wasn't a nose and didn't have the qualities required. Pierre not only had *le nez*, he had the compassion and commitment to the raw product; to the romance of the dance of perfume.

'I can't believe your company does that, Henri,' she said as he grasped her hand and walked her towards the terrace over-looking the pool.

He shushed her like a child. 'It's business, Kitty. The prices of imported flowers are much lower. It makes sound commercial sense.'

She wanted to rip her hand out of his grip. 'But you know that the conditions of the workers picking flowers in those countries is appalling. They're lowly paid, suffer terrible conditions and worse, they probably use children.' She shuddered.

'Let's not fight. I have my mother's dinner tonight, but I've slipped away to see you.'

He caressed her hand and resisted when she tried to pull it away.

'Sorry to interrupt.' Sofia delivered two aperitifs. 'Courtesy of Adrienne.'

Henri kissed Kitty's forehead and stepped back to sip his drink before leading her to a nearby table and they sat, their knees touching.

'I've been thinking about you a lot,' he commenced.

'Do you want to learn more about my perfume idea?'

'Yes,' but he hesitated and Kitty wasn't convinced. 'Soon. First, I want to tell you about an exciting opportunity.' Kitty inched closer. 'My sister is getting married and moving to Switzerland. Her husband's passion is not perfume and they are moving for his work. Therefore,' he dragged out the syllables. 'There is a position vacant in the company.' He clasped her hands in his and held them in his lap, 'And I think it would be perfect for you.'

A thousand thoughts slammed into her brain at the same

time and she lost her coherent ability to think. Recovering, she asked, 'What is the position?'

'You have a passion for perfume, and that is exactly what we need in our company. Someone who can sell with authenticity and tell the consumer about the intricate elements of the perfume and about the process.'

'O-k-a-y...but what would I be doing?'

'One of the most important positions in the business. Front of house. You would be involved in not only selling the perfume but in marketing and design and publicity...'

'The shop?' A cavern of deep disappointment opened in her chest. 'I thought you understood my passion was for creating perfume?'

'I do, I do, sweet Kitty. But no one starts in their dream job. You'd need to work your way into the lab. You can learn on the job and eventually fulfil your dream. Or perhaps your dreams might even change over time.' He was looking at her in a funny way, his head cocked, a crooked grin lifting his mouth.

Deja vu hit her square in the chest. She'd heard these words before. Kitty gulped her drink.

'I can see you're unsure, it's a big decision moving from Australia to live here in France.'

That's why he thought she hesitated?

'I was going to wait, but it might help you decide.' He grinned and his expression morphed into something else. His eyes were wide open like a child expressing excitement, and his lips parted, his pearly white teeth on display.

He pulled a box out of his pocket. It was small, square and blue. Opening the lid revealed a sparkling oval blue sapphire stone in a plain gold band with tiny offset diamonds on each side of the centre stone. He knelt on one knee, got out his handkerchief and mopped his sweating brow before focusing his attention on her. A gust of wind blew strands of hair into her face and a ringing commenced in her ears. 'Kitty Landers from Australia, I have enjoyed getting to know you. You have been a breath of fresh air. I know we could be wonderful together, make a great team and achieve amazing things. My family like you, they say we are a good match. That you are reliable and committed and pretty. I'd like our relationship to continue in both life and perfume. Will you marry me?'

Henri left and Kitty strode towards the house, her only thought of another drink, maybe lots more drinks.

Inside Adrienne was in the kitchen. Kitty found the bottle of tequila on the top shelf and gestured to Adrienne who nodded. The house mistress watched her pour two shots. Kitty drank hers in one gulp before pouring another.

'Sit down my pet. What's up?'

Kitty didn't mean to, didn't want to, but she cried big, fat, ugly tears. Adrienne pulled her in close, and she sobbed harder. It was nice to be held and comforted. She'd missed a lot of that growing up, and she'd been searching for love ever since. The stupid romantic in her, but why was she upset now when she didn't believe in that happy-ever-after stuff anymore anyway?

'Henri asked me to marry him.'

Adrienne's eyebrows shot up, and she drank her shot and then poured them another. Kitty laughed, and her tears dried up. 'Yes, exactly, that's my reaction, too.'

'Do you love him?'

'We don't even know each other!' As it sank in, the idea seemed preposterous to her. She kept replaying Henri's words in her head. He hadn't said he loved her, hadn't uttered any words of adoration. It had sounded like a business transaction. Maybe that was okay? She barrelled on. 'Is it always about love, Adrienne? Can you be with someone for safety, security, companionship?'

Kitty caught the expression that flittered across Adrienne's face before she controlled it. She guessed she had her answer. But of course, a Frenchwoman madly in love with her husband would think that, right?

'Those are very admirable aspirations, I agree,' she said, speaking slowly, appearing to make up her response as she went along and clearly struggling.

'Let me tell you this first.' Kitty roughly wiped her wet cheeks. 'In Australia, my fiancé was part of a successful perfume house. We met when I commenced working in their shop as a retail assistant. I'd never encountered perfume before and I fell in love. I adored the smells, and once I understood the ingredients, I could identify the different fragrances. I devoured the packaging, read articles and learned as much as I could. My employer thought my interest was delightful. Stuart, the son of the owners, and I fell in love and I thought I was going to become a creator and learn from them, be part of their future, their dynasty. I was thrilled. But they never delivered on the promise. They made excuses: sales were down, the technicians were too busy to teach me, ingredients and stock was low, it was endless. I hoped after we married, they would make good on my wish. Of course, I never married, and that dream was lost.' She drank another shot, and the liquid warmed her inside.

'Henri offered me a job in his perfume house, too and made similar promises. Adrienne, how freaky is that? Am I only ever destined to be a shop girl? Is this the world telling me that's all I'm capable of?'

'No, don't be ridiculous!' Adrienne jumped in so quickly with the reassurance that Kitty was buoyed.

'He's very handsome. He's kind to me. I like him, he comes from a large and loving family with a thriving perfume business. He's handsome,' she repeated.

'Sounds like you are trying to convince yourself. I don't know a lot, my love, but I think any woman knows when they want to be with someone. It doesn't come down to pros and cons, does it? Love is love. You know in here.' She pressed her hand to Kitty's heart.

Kitty sighed. 'I would have agreed once, but I made the wrong choice, thought I had found the person I loved and could spend the rest of my life with, but that didn't work. I'm afraid my judgment now is off...and I might make the wrong decision.'

'Your judgment isn't off, *ma cherie*. You loved Stuart, those feelings were true. Unfortunately, for whatever reason, he didn't return your love. It doesn't mean it was wrong or bad or that you made a mistake. Perhaps he made a mistake?'

Adrienne poured her a glass of water and then took the bottle, returned it to the shelf and continued the dinner preparations. Kitty wandered back outside.

It was so beautiful here. It might be the most perfect place in the world. The people were attractive and glamorous, and the setting was stunning. Out here on the terrace, the pool shimmered, a breeze blew and in the distance the sun was beginning its descent into night. The twinkling lights of Grasse were the backdrop. It was swoon worthy romantic.

Ironically, Henri's proposal had been lovely, better than her first. And Henri Beaumont would make a wonderful husband. He was a man to marry, then why wouldn't she? It made sense and would secure her a future in the perfume industry.

She did like him, but he didn't animate her like someone else…an image of Pierre popped into her head. Now, that was a man not to marry. Dangerous, too damn good-looking, adverse to any sort of commitment, out of her league and was destined to break every girl's heart. It was ludicrous to place the word marry and Pierre in the same sentence.

The prospect of staying in Grasse excited Kitty. She'd found her life's passion. Knew now that perfume was her future. And everyone in the town loved perfume, even if they were not involved in the industry. Like Raph and Adrienne, their accommodation blossomed because of the tourist trade brought by perfume. The hills were surrounded by flowers in bloom and fragrances in the air. The shops were filled with associated perfume products.

Kitty hoped her future was not in selling perfume to tourists and the rich and famous of Europe. She had to make her dream happen.

And love, bloody love. She no longer knew where that fitted in or what she believed anymore. France had taught her love existed in different forms. The French people kissed and hugged in the street, swooned, and took acts of romanticism seriously. They not only oozed *l'amour*, but passion.

Wasn't she yet cured of this thing called love? And if that

were true, Henri would be perfect. But...but... Kitty sank into a deck chair. Yes, she wanted to be cured, but feared deep down, she wasn't. Because she knew she'd defer logic and not accept Henri's proposal, she couldn't, wouldn't. And what did that really mean?

She'd fled to France to pursue her dreams. Not to find love. Right?

Chapter Seventeen

Entering the farm, Kitty knew straight away. The air was fresh, the world wet. The rain had pelted down during the night, heavy and unrelenting. On the short ride to Pierre's fields, boughs covered roads and leaves were scattered across paths.

What should have been yet another busy morning harvesting the rose centifolia, she was instead met with silence. No chatting or last-minute frivolities, not any of the usual rush to prepare. Instead, the group took their last sip of their espressos and then donned their aprons.

Kitty walked straight to the field, soil squelching under her feet, and saw the carnage: limp plants and bushes, bent and broken branches, once perfect blossoms missing their petals, torn leaves either hanging precariously or strewn messily around the bases. At the first bush in the row, she bowed her head, and the scent was still evident, but the flowers looked bruised, the plant sad, and destroyed.

It wasn't Pierre who spoke. Another fellow she recognised from daily picking took charge, his expression grim. 'Today is clean up and salvage. Some blooms may have survived, perhaps hidden or protected by the plants or other leaves. Those will be picked. Otherwise, our job is to tidy up the fields. Rake the leaves, tender to broken stalks.' he demonstrated, 'and remove damaged leaves and branches. With our help, the plants can survive for tomorrow and the remainder of the picking.' The man wiped his brow; already the sun held heat and blanketed them in humidity. It might be a blessing. The warmth would soak up the moisture and dry out the soil.

A deep pain seared Kitty's chest. She turned away, not having the stomach for harvesting a ruined crop. She snuck away. Arriving inside the shed, she relished the cool and proceeded to the lab before pulling up short at the entrance. A thumping sound emanated from within. Taking one further step, she saw them.

Pierre stood at the far wall, his back to her. Between his legs, she glimpsed flesh, a long, lean, bare leg wearing a wedged heel. The other leg was off the ground, held gripped in his hand, the foot curled around his leg. His other large hand was flat to the wall, pinning them in place.

She gasped and the leg dropped. Pierre's head turned enough to glimpse her in the doorway. The woman sashayed out from behind him, tidied her dress and wiped the corners of her mouth.

Kitty turned and fled. Footsteps hurried behind her, and an arm tugged at her elbow, forcing her to stop. Pierre yanked her around to face him, his eyes ablaze. He leaned forwards, cupped her face in his hands and kissed her. It was impossible to do anything but melt at his touch. She'd been dreaming of more ever since the other night...but not like this. The rebound: the afterthought when his passion was already burning for someone else.

His lips caressed her bare shoulder, brushed aside the strap and kissed the soft skin there. Despite herself, she let him and gripped a hand to his waist and moved him closer, his arousal obvious. Oh, she wanted more. A noise sounded behind her, and the world crashed down upon them. The other woman scurried out of the room with her head down. It was like a blowtorch to her fire. What was she doing? What the hell was he doing? Kitty placed her two palms to Pierre's chest and pushed him away. He was still dressed in last night's clothes with his tie askew.

'Urgh! Don't touch me!'

She slid sideways and away from him, rushed to the workbench and retrieved her vial. Pierre was behind her in a flash and snatched the vial from her hand. He uncapped the lid and inhaled, performed an exaggerated intake of breath. Did this man never stop?

'What is this?'

Kitty's chest heaved. 'I made it.'

'This?' He questioned. She didn't reply and he checked the scent again, bowed his head. Was he drunk?

'What?' she was defensive now.

'Kitty. Kitty.'

He was patronising her now?

'You can do better than this. New creations must be original and innovative. This is similar to every perfume Beaumont has ever produced...'

Beaumont? He had to be kidding. The truth was she thought *Beaumont de Villiers* perfume was disgusting. So, he was insulting her perfume, the one she'd created. The one where she'd thought she'd cracked it and made something different. She had done exactly as he'd taught; there was story and purpose to it. She'd made it from her heart, hadn't she?

'I thought it was...good...' That familiar self-doubt burst through her.

'Good.' He sneered. 'Good is not enough. Good is for amateurs.'

'Pierre, teach me then... make me the best...I can do it. You know I can...' She started out strong, but she pleaded now. 'Please.'

'A perfumer is born. Perfume is a tradition, an industry based on generations of experience. You can't learn it, be taught, it lives in here.' He touched her chest with a lone finger where her heart lay underneath. 'Even when you don't want it...it is not a job you apply for.'

'I thought you said I was talented, was a natural...' Her voice was a whisper.

Pierre laughed then, and it sliced her in two. The sound was bitter and cruel and rang in her ears. Her legs went weak.

What was wrong with him? She stared at him but he refused to meet her eye; he glanced down at his feet, eyes darting sideways to the vial.

'Are you being honest? Are you saying that there is no chance that I will ever be a perfumer, no matter what I do, how much I learn, how much I practise?' Pause. 'That I am not *le nez*?' Kitty held her breath.

Pierre lifted his head, jutted his chin, his gaze steely and unwavering. 'Yes.'

She ran and didn't look back. Tears pooled in her eyes and blinded her. Swiping them away roughly, she reached the bike at the gates of the farm and was about to jump on when Pierre gripped the handlebars. That man was fast.

'No, you can't ride.'

She tried to pull the bike from his grip. He held fast, and she tried again, their arms pushing and pulling. Kitty stomped on his foot, forcing him to release the bike. It swayed. Taking her chance, she grabbed the bars with two hands and ran, swinging her legs over the seat while moving. She'd done that trick a million times as a kid.

'Kitty! No!' His yell was anguished. Not nearly as anguished as she felt right now. Pierre Joubert was like everyone else and thought she was a joke. Obviously, his compliments were only to get her into bed or to fall in love with him. Fall for his charm like every other woman. Damn him. The wind whipped her tears away as she rode as fast as she could.

Metres down the steep hill, she slowed her pedalling, thinking she'd escaped, when she heard a whir behind her. Glancing back, she saw Pierre advancing on another bicycle. His face was white, his hands gripping the handlebars tightly as the pedals turned without his legs and sped down the hill.

Oh, Pierre. Memories of his brother and his accident flooded back to her. She kept checking behind her to make sure he was okay when she lost attention. Something on the road caught in her wheel, the bike wobbled and she tumbled.

'Kitty!' The words rang out as she hit the hard concrete.

The thump as she connected with the ground winded her and she lay motionless. Pierre was beside her in an instant.

'Kitty! Kitty!' Quickly regaining her wits, she pulled herself up. 'Get away from me!' His touch repulsed her now. She shoved at his chest until he landed on his backside on the road. Picking up the bike, she said a silent prayer of thanks it had remained intact. She swung her legs over once more and rode away as fast as her heavy legs would allow.

Each turn of the pedal caused an ache to shoot up her legs. Her hands were heavy on the bars while blood trickled down her shins. The tears weren't from injury but flowed freely on her return ride to the villa. Head down, focusing on reaching her destination, she didn't see the two men standing outside. But she smelled them. Her head jerked up as the scent drifted towards her. Magnolia. An aroma she'd once loved. It couldn't be...

That perfume was like going home.

Light and fruity, the scent belonged to Stuart of *Montgomery Perfumes*.

'Kitty?' His face was etched with concern and he rushed towards her. Stuart returning to her was something she'd dreamed a lot in the early days of her arrival in Grasse. She blinked a couple of times. It really was him. Perhaps if the perfume of him wasn't so strong, she wouldn't believe it, but his arms around her confirmed it was not an hallucination. Stuart was in Grasse, France. A long way from Australia.

Why was he here?

Kitty fell into his arms, her legs giving way, her resilience running low after the last few days.

Then she immediately berated herself, came to her senses and batted his hands away. She'd been strong and had handled stressful situations since she'd left home and the moment her ex-fiancé turns up, she crumbles? Ridiculous.

Standing back, she observed Andy, Stuart's best friend, standing with him. She held her hand up in greeting. He approached and kissed her on the cheek, 'Hi, Kitty.'

Kitty took them both in. Stuart with his short blonde hair remained boyishly cute. His dimple was prominent on his left cheek. He'd lost weight; a sign of his distress? Of his mistake in dumping her at the altar? Was he here to get her back? Despite the passage of time over the last few weeks, hope flared in her chest like little firecrackers going off. He wanted her back! He'd finally realised he'd made a mistake; he still loved her.

As she daydreamed, Stuart stepped in beside Andy and placed his arm around his shoulders. 'Kitty, we need to talk.'

Huh! Kitty rubbed her scratchy eyes. The two men glanced at each other. The kitchen door opened and shut behind her, and the girls from the villa rushed out.

'Kitty! We told him to go away, that famous and rich perfumers were courting you. We told him what for...' Julia, Sofia and Marianne talked at once. They were defending her; these girls who'd thought in the beginning she was stupid and not made out to be a perfumer in her own right were sticking up for her. Kitty realised in a flash that they had become her friends. They circled Stuart and Andy, and she welled up with happiness but hushed them.

'It's okay. Thank you for looking out for me, but I guess I

have to listen to what he has to say.' She glanced, uncertain, then at Stuart and Andy, who still stood with their arms entwined. Her thoughts were in disarray.

Next, Adrienne and Raph rushed out with glasses in their hands, Adrienne carried a bottle. 'Ah, Kitty, you have visitors.' Adrienne's eyes were full of questions, her brows raised. 'Come, sit on the terrace, you can talk, drink,' she held up the alcohol, 'and we'll bring some, what you say in Australia, nibbles?' The older woman laughed, breaking the tension that had been mounting.

Kitty nodded. Yes, a drink on the terrace. Civilised.

No one spoke as they settled, Adrienne fussing, filling glasses, making introductions, and small talk. She gave Kitty a pointed stare, asking if she was okay. Kitty nodded, and her heart swelled again. Adrienne was a friend, too.

Stuart launched immediately into apologies, he was so sorry, it was unforgivable what he'd done. He was embarrassed at his actions. He hoped she could forgive him. Then he reached across and clasped Andy's hand and held it in his lap. 'I'm in love with someone else. I'm so sorry that you were dragged into the mess of my life. But the thing is, Kitty, that I'm, well, I love Andy.'

The air around Kitty electrified and zapped, intensifying her inner emotions. The sinking sun became too hot, and the stars only just revealing themselves became startlingly bright. The world around her shifted. 'As a friend, you mean?' Her eyes darted between them. She loved Andy, too; he had been a great pal during the years of her relationship with Stuart.

'Kitty, I'm gay. I thought I could make it work with you. Make my parents happy, and we could live a normal life. But I couldn't. Can't. I love Andy, and we have exciting news. We got married on our way here. Andy is my husband.'

The words sank in. 'You're gay?' Her voice quavered.

He nodded.

'Did you ever love me?'

More zealous nodding. 'Yes, I did, you were a great friend, I cared for you deeply. We were a great team, but my heart wasn't in it. You deserved better, someone to really love you.'

Hell, yes, she did. And she thought that person was Stuart. But he was gay. And she never knew. 'You deceived me?'

He hung his head then. 'Yes, but it wasn't only you. I deceived everyone. My parents didn't know either. It's no excuse, but I was living a lie, living a life everyone else wanted me to lead. I tried, really, to make it work with you. I thought for a while it might be enough, but it wasn't...'

A scream welled up within her. They had been together for five years! That was a lot of pretending.

Sudden realisation hit her. It wasn't her. Like in the movies and romance novels, it was him. Stuart didn't like women. So, therefore, by conclusion, he couldn't love her. He'd tried, but he preferred men. She raised her head and stared at them both. They made a cute couple. But he'd still deceived her. Lifting her left hand, she slapped him across the face.

He didn't flinch; Andy placed a hand on Stuart's knee.

'I'm really happy for you,' she said and burst into tears.

Stuart and Andy dined with them that night at the villa. It was like a party with friends.

Adrienne prepared a feast and Raph provided *le vin*. The students were good company boasting about Kitty's development since her arrival. Saying she'd learned a lot and was now officially a perfumer in training.

Kitty ignored the pang in her chest but did not correct them. They quizzed Stuart about his family company and he answered with pride. It was their intention to return to Australia and work together in the business. A piece of her heart did crack and drop away at the comment, but she saw how happy Stuart was and thought back to more recent times. Had he been restrained? Unhappy? She hadn't thought so, but her own happiness must have blinded her.

Kitty sat back and watched the interaction as relief washed over her, satisfied that Stuart had had the strength to reveal his secret and travel across the world in person to tell her. To make sure she was okay. He was a good guy; her judgment hadn't been off entirely. Stuart Montgomery deserved to be happy with Andy. Finally, their relationship was out in the open. The French accepted any form of love, so there'd be little opposition here. She wasn't so sure about the Montgomery family, but Kitty knew they loved their son and she hoped that would be enough.

Sitting on the terrace in the balmy summer evening, the chatter of those around her muted into the background. She dwelled on Pierre and his comments. The one person in Grasse who had supported her revealed her dream was an impossible one. She'd never be a perfumer, regardless of how well she could smell.

Her greatest fear had come true. Now, she had nothing.

Chapter Eighteen

Clarity hit Pierre hard. He'd gotten too close to Kitty. That night, he'd revealed too much. That was the first sign, he never spoke of his brother's death, ever. Then at the home, watching Kitty with Claude and the other children. For the first time he could recall, he'd seen a future...with her.

Kitty was a good person, but his feelings for her had morphed into something he couldn't even describe. They were so foreign to him that they caused an ache to spread across his chest so much that it hurt.

And for that reason, Pierre needed to set her free before anything happened, before he slept with her, even though he wanted nothing more. And worse, before she fell in love with him. It was too great a risk. Kitty deserved better than a man who could not commit, who hurt those he loved the most.

Remembering the pain on her face when he'd lied to her caused a fresh wave of anguish to wash through him.

'C'mon, love. Come and have a drink with an old lady,' Mrs

Roubillard said to Pierre as he inspected yet another rose bush in the dying dusk of the day.

'I think they've survived well, don't you?' she asked as Pierre reluctantly left the field and his thoughts behind.

'Yes, I've been lucky. That rainstorm could have wiped out the entire harvest, but most of it will be salvaged. A few damaged blooms and more than I'd like, but it's not as catastrophic as I first thought.' He offered a weak smile and accepted the drink she presented and followed her to the terrace.

'No romantic interlude tonight?' he asked her as they sat.

'Not tonight. Andreas is with his wife.'

'Do you ever tire of sharing him?' Pierre had never asked and even though he considered himself a forward-thinking French-man; it was not a situation he envied.

'No, but if I get lonely, I have you.' She smiled coquettishly in his direction.

'I'm terrible company. The home is threatened. They might shut us down if I don't find a solution and my harvest was near ruin...' He let the words hang.

'Sounds like there is more than that?'

A car rumbled on the drive. His mother parked and got out of her metallic silver Austin Martin. Mrs Roubillard rose and waited until Mrs Joubert arrived on the terrace. 'Please, Marie, sit. I will join you. It's a beautiful evening,' his mother said in greeting.

Pierre accepted his mother's kisses.

'I wanted to drop by and let you know some exciting news.' As usual, his mother had no time for pleasantries. Pierre waited. *Jardin d'Amour* has been awarded best new fragrance of the year. Isn't that wonderful?'

'*C'est magnifique!*' Pierre declared. The first piece of good news he'd heard recently. A reward for the hard work of their chemists and testers and their entire team. It was a huge achievement. His chest swelled with pride like a parent proud of their child. And, of course, it was good for business, too.

'There is no mistaking, darling, this is a result of your dedication and devotion to the brand.'

Pierre choked, his cognac almost coming back up.

'Our award is going to feature in a special advertisement before the main screening at the Cannes Film Festival. Plus, it's outselling some of our long-term favourites.'

Mrs Roubillard tapped his hand in a motherly fashion.

'Marie, this calls for champagne, let's celebrate.'

Dutifully, Mrs Roubillard obeyed and moved away to fetch the drinks.

His mother's words were jovial but her actions stilted.

'It's wonderful news, Mother. This exposure will catapult our perfume out into the world.'

Pierre, while ecstatic for the perfume award, was guarded. It was unusual for his mother to share such news in person and more to praise him. When she placed her gnarled and worn hand over his, his gut knotted. Displays of affection never occurred either.

'You do wonderful work at the company, and your father, and I appreciate what you do.' She stumbled as if the words were difficult to form. She avoided his eye but continued. 'I know we are short on compliments and don't always express ourselves the way we should. But you taking over and running the business has allowed us to step back from the years of unrelenting focus and develop other interests and form some semblance of a life together.'

Pierre's anxiety increased.

'It's important to say these things now and tell you.' His mother's body language, with gripped and tight knuckles in her lap, indicated it wasn't easy for her.

'Now?' he queried. 'What's wrong, mother?' The knot in his stomach tightened.

'Your father is unwell. It's come on rather suddenly, and his illness has made me realise that if I lose him, there's only you and me, and we need to take care of one another.' Her voice cracked.

'What can I do?'

A tight smile touched her lips. 'Nothing, nothing. He is receiving the best medical care.' Her words dripped with sarcasm. As if, once again, she found herself in a situation that money couldn't fix. Like years ago, at the death of his brother. If they could have, they would have sacrificed anything, paid any amount of money, to have Louis back, he knew that. 'He might come good, we'll see.' She shook her head as if banishing those thoughts. She divulged the true nature of his condition and Pierre listened.

The air around them felt heavy now rather than celebratory.

Mrs Joubert gazed into the distance as she continued to speak. 'I do know you have harboured resentment all these years. You believe that we abandoned you and didn't care for you as the son that we should have.'

More revelations. Pierre was on high alert.

'You can't understand what it's like to lose a son. You will never until one day, perhaps, when you have your own children. It is not only devastating but soul-destroying. And we blamed ourselves.' She looked at him then, directly, perhaps for the first time.

Pierre turned away first and sat back, reeling.

'Yes, yes we did.' His mother became more animated now and fidgeted in her seat. 'We worked too hard, were absent, and left both of you in the care of others. We thought it was the right thing to do; we had a multi-million-dollar business to run and a legacy to continue and we couldn't stop. And then... then something awful happens and everything changes. But I need you to understand that we were wrong about many things, but we cannot take that back now. After Louis died, we were desperate to keep you safe. We couldn't bear to have anything happen to our only surviving son. But we couldn't stop working; we had to keep making the perfume, so we thought the best option to keep you safe was boarding school. The school would look after you like we could not. You were under constant supervision and getting a top-class education as an added bonus. It seemed like the perfect solution.'

Pierre willed himself not to cry and formed his words. 'You sent me away to keep me safe?'

His mother nodded and wrung a handkerchief through her fingers.

Pierre shook his head, kept it bowed, eyes off his mother. 'I thought it was because you blamed me, couldn't stand the sight of me, banished me for killing Louis.'

His mother hitched a sob, but she maintained her composure. 'It was never like that. I can see in retrospect that our decision was unwise. It alienated you, increased the distance between us. Yes, you were safe but I didn't understand then that you might have perhaps needed us. I didn't understand that you blamed yourself and grieved like we did. Plus,' her voice cracked, 'we didn't know what to say. Couldn't say the right things. We were so distraught and nothing we did could make it right. So, for everything, I'm sorry. It has taken the prospect of losing your father for me to realise, to remember...and have the courage to say that I love you, appreciate the work you're doing and I'm sorry. I fear too much has happened since, and we cannot make amends, but nonetheless, I need to say these things to you. If your father does not recover,' her voice lost further composure and caught on a sob, 'it will be you and me against the world.'

Silence lingered heavy on the deck. His mother was the first to fill the void.

'It also took me a long time to realise that you operate Rose House to make amends, but you have nothing to make amends for. You've lived a wonderful full life of service to others. You have run this company better than your father. The recent years have been wonderful, the brand of *House of Joubert* has never been stronger. You make beautiful perfume. Plus, you save those beautiful needy children.'

Mrs Roubillard returned with a bottle of champagne and flutes. She poured. 'Please join us, Marie,' his mother said.

'*Non*, Mrs Joubert, you enjoy talking with your son.' Mrs Roubillard gave Pierre a meaningful glare. He said a silent prayer back, promising not to mess this up.

They clinked glasses in a very civilised manner and sipped the delicate French drop.

'May I give you some advice, dear? I know I've not been the most maternal guiding light, but hear me out. I understand there is an issue at the home, and I have the perfect solution. First, though, I think you need to learn that you do not have to save every child, and it is not your job to find each of them a loving home, but...I've seen you with the boy.'

'Claude?' Pierre was still catching up with the change of track in their conversation.

'Yes. Claude. The solution is simple. There's a wonderful loving home here for him. Why don't you adopt him?'

Adopt Claude? The idea was preposterous. What did he have to offer a ten-year-old kid?

'You and Father would approve of me adopting a child who wasn't of our own blood? That wasn't of French class and old money and from the right part of society? Plus wasn't a nose?' His mother flinched.

'It is the right thing to do.'

'Yes, but do I then adopt every child that can't stay at the home? The situation could get out of hand.'

'Well, you deal with this problem first and then advocate to expand the home to take more children or seek to amend the regulations or some such thing I would imagine?'

It was a brilliant idea, but Pierre feared he couldn't keep Claude safe. Like his mother and father had sent him away, Pierre worried that Claude was safest at the home, out of his direct care. But...could she be right?

If that was possible, were other things he'd previously considered impossible, also achievable? If he could keep Claude safe, could he keep himself and others safe too? Love other people? Let them in?

Had he made a grave mistake in pushing away Kitty? Had he

acted like his parents? One of the things he vowed never to do. And could he make it right?

'Mother, there's something else I'd really like to do.'

'Oh, I'm intrigued. Refill our glasses first.'

Chapter Nineteen

Andy and Stuart played out an advertisement for true love in front of her as she sat across from them at a local café the next morning.

The two men adored one another; did those annoying things people in love did: finished each other's sentences, smiled constantly at the other when they thought no one was looking, touched hands and knees under the table thinking no one would notice and fed each other bits of their breakfast.

But their relationship was way more than those gestures. She observed commitment, devotion, exclusivity—much to the chagrin of the French around her probably— pure joy, a sense of safety, their invincibleness as a couple. She was in awe of the power it evoked.

Only a few short weeks ago, Kitty would have scoffed at the scene or fallen into a pit of jealousy.

Now, oh boy, she envied them. Overnight, her anger at Stuart had dissipated. Yes, he'd done the wrong thing, lied to her and everyone, but she understood. Coming out as gay was tough, and she admired his bravery.

And most of all, it was a relief, a burden lifted from her shoulders. Until now, she'd carried around the sense that she'd done something wrong, and was unlovable because Stuart rejected her. That wasn't true. Plus, she had to accept, finally, that love did exist, and she guessed she needed to find it.

The loved-up pair in front of her didn't realise they'd restored her faith in love. Unfortunately, with that epiphany, she was not scared. It was easy to swear off love and romanticism—safe, certain. Being the Scrooge of love was sort of fun and easy, leaving you without qualms and endless sleepless nights wondering where you stood.

Andy and Stuart had it; Adrienne and Raph, too.

And yet, despite her resolve, she remained very much alone.

Thoughts of Pierre and her lost perfume career drifted in, but she shoved them away.

To avoid the lovefest, she glanced away across the square. Maybe she'd simply fall in love with Grasse, that was easy. She had grown to adore this town but what pull did it have without the perfume?

Coming out of a café across the terraced square with espresso coffees in hand, was Henri. With a woman. A twinge squeezed her heart, but it was fleeting. The couple linked arms and smiled broad grins at each other, the ones only affectionate people shared. The woman was all bronzed legs and brown hair and wearing a mini-dress barely covering her thighs. But, hell, if you had legs like that you needed to show them off. He was speaking to her and the woman was hanging off his every word. Henri lapped up the attention.

Kitty waited for the emotion to hit. Betrayal? Disappointment? Rejection? She felt nothing.

From the moment Henri had uttered his affections, followed by his expectations, they'd weighed heavily on her. And she hadn't realised how much. Deep down, she'd known. But Kitty had also suffered lack of belief in her decision-making, but glancing across at Stuart, that needed to change, now. Stuart had never been an option, and now she understood Henri wasn't either.

So, she'd refused his proposal. It had shocked him. But watching him now was a revelation for her: if Henri was her one, her heart would be breaking watching him with another woman. She'd be deeply hurt and filled with humiliation and embarrassment at being forgotten. When, in fact, she felt the opposite: relieved, and that could only mean one thing: Henri wasn't for her. He wasn't *the one*, even though she wasn't sure she subscribed to that philosophy one hundred percent anymore.

Instead, she wished him well. It would appear in typical French fashion he had bounced back, and quickly. Every person deserved to be the rapture of someone's attention. Like Andy and Stuart. Like Adrienne listened when Raph talked.

Perhaps she didn't believe in love being a fairy tale of happily ever after anymore, but she still desired the romanticism of it: flowers, chocolates, devotion, rapturous attention, that safety of being cared for and the ongoing long-term commitment. In this moment, she declared to herself, that she would not sacrifice nor accept anything less.

'Get in.'

'No.' Kitty's reply was short and sharp. She kept walking. Pierre's car rumbled slowly past her on the streets of Grasse.

He inched forward and stopped the car. 'We need to talk. Please let me explain. It's not what you think.'

'Isn't it?' Kitty paused and leaned through the passenger window. He took that as a good sign. 'You have no faith in me, I have no future in perfume. You stomped on my dreams. That about sums it up.'

'I can explain, but you need to get in,' he revved the engine. Hopefully, she couldn't see him gripping the steering wheel so hard that his knuckles turned white.

She took her sweet time but opened the door and hopped in the passenger seat. Pierre sped away lest Kitty change her mind.

The silence in the car was deadly, so he drove fast. Lucky, it was a quick trip, and soon, he pulled the Ferrari into his designated spot at the *House of Joubert* premises and factory. Kitty darted a look across at him, which he ignored but raced around to open her door.

Her face was a myriad of expressions, and he let the corners of his lips lift in confidence. It must have taken all Kitty's self-control to hold her tongue; on the outside she was perfectly composed.

He entered through the front door. It was important Kitty saw the entire production of the factory: the entry and foyer, the corridors, the staff at work, the lab and the real heart of the *House of Joubert*. Pierre glanced at her and was buoyed by her wide-eyed reaction. This was exactly what he wanted. This was a special place and he was glad she thought so too. And she knew that no one entered the den of the house unless you worked here. It was sacred ground.

His adrenalin spiked. A lot depended on how this went. But he needed to stay focused on business first instead of his desire to sweep this gorgeous Australian girl off her feet and whisk her away to some of the most glamorous places on the Cote D'Azur. That was where you wooed a woman, the glitz, the glamour, the scenery stole people's hearts on a daily basis. He could have. But not yet, they needed to talk. Kitty was not a woman easily duped. He hoped he was right.

In the lab and workroom, he commenced his elaborate spiel about the process and production. He allowed her to smell various works in progress, chat with the chemists and examine the elements of the room. It was a much larger version of his home lab.

Roughly halfway through she seemed to forget her anger at him and soaked up every word, every scent and the experience. He slowed to her pace and saw her soften, come alive. This was where she belonged. Hope flared.

One of their experienced chemists approached him to seek his opinion on a fragrance she'd been working on. Kitty was by his side in an instant.

'This is new, *oui*?'

The chemist confirmed it was.

'We have been working on a different scent, less floral, less Joubert. It's a special project,' the chemist informed him.

He hadn't tested any of these combinations yet. 'Close your eyes,' he directed Kitty and when she complied, he placed a small strip tester to her nose. She inhaled, once, twice, but she kept her eyes shut before opening them and reaching for the bottle.

'What do you detect?' he asked her. Pierre noticed the chemist's shift of feet, the sway of her stance.

'The top note is burnt orange...

The chemist interrupted, 'Bitter orange...'

Kitty kept going undeterred. 'And ginger. Heart note is definitely patouchli, and there is cedarwood and musk, but there is one I cannot name.' Her forehead creased into a frown.

'Yes, that one is hard. It is tonka bean, and it's a real combination of elements, so it's hard to decipher. It's a mixture of vanilla, tobacco, gourmand and almond mixed with a bit of ginger and wood which is already present, so hard to pick up.'

Kitty took the vial again and inhaled, nodding. To the chemist, he said, 'Can you get some pure tonka bean, please?' When the chemist returned, Pierre gave it to Kitty to engross herself in the scent. She offered it back. He shook his head. 'Keep it.'

Holding up the essence, he addressed the chemist. 'I think you've really succeeded in making something different to our usual scents. This screams oriental essences of the East. It is heavier, darker, and exudes strength and depth. All characteristics distinguishable to that part of the world.'

'Yes, spicy, and strong like the heat,' Kitty added. Pierre smiled. The chemist nodded, also impressed.

Pierre extracted Kitty's labelled vial from his pocket and gave it to the chemist. 'Tell me what you think of this.' Kitty's chest inflated as if she was inhaling; she also fidgeted with her hands.

Like any good perfumer, the chemist took their time to digest the smell and understand the scent. 'This is different, too,' she said. 'Not anything like this one,' she pointed to her creation. 'Opposite in fact. This is fresh, light like citrus but with undertones of the sea.'

Kitty shifted her feet. Pierre was aware that the chemist had detected the essence of the fragrance and had conjured up the sensation Kitty had hoped for.

'But not sophisticated, nor finished...' the chemist added.

'Ms Landers created this scent,' Pierre said.

'Ms Landers, it is a great attempt and with refinement I think it can be great.'

Lost for words, Kitty glowed in the praise.

Pierre nodded and the chemist was dismissed. 'Let's go to my office.' He guided her through the narrow corridors to the far reach of the building. Inside, he offered coffee, tea or something stronger while gesturing to the fully stocked bar in the corner with any drink one's heart could desire. And he'd desired many over his time.

'It's only mid-morning,' she exclaimed.

'Whatever you want.'

She asked for a coffee. He made the order through an intercom system.

'Kitty.' He kneeled in front of the chair where she sat. 'I am so sorry for what I said the other day. I didn't mean it, well no, sorry I did. It is true that perfume is a tradition and birthright, and all those things, but it is not true that one cannot be trained, one's skills honed.'

He sat forward to grasp her hands. 'Truth is, I was scared. Scared that you didn't belong here, you are innocent, kind and honest and this is a tough industry. I was scared my parents wouldn't allow me to buck generations of tradition. It might take years to be the best. But I think you can do it. My parents understand I'm in charge and support my decisions. I can do as I wish, change direction, we can do things differently in the future.'

Thank you, Mother, he said to himself, for granting permission, agreeing it was a fabulous idea.

Kitty looked at him quizzically.

'I knew that I couldn't hire you as a chemist to train you to be a perfumer. It was not allowed, not the done thing, would expose us as amateurs if we did not follow tradition. But like the world around us, things change. There is always room for people with talent and *le nez.* Kitty Landers, I would like you to come and work here at the *House of Joubert.*'

She blinked. 'In the shop?'

'What? The shop? As in selling perfume to tourists?' He shook his head. 'No, why would I want you in the shop? I have wonderful retail staff.'

Kitty still looked blank. 'I want you to become one of the most wonderful creators of perfume the *House of Joubert* has ever had. I have enormous confidence in your talent. With the right training and practice, you will be brilliant.'

Their coffees arrived, and Pierre waited, hardly daring to breathe.

Kitty was silent. A thousand thoughts fought for space in his head.

'I don't understand what has changed.'

'I was wrong. What you have created so far with your rudimentary knowledge is wonderful, classy perfume.'

'You think I'm talented? Say it again.'

'The truth is Kitty; I made a mistake. I was scared,' he repeated.

Eyes focused intently on his, she interrupted. 'So, you want me to work for you to create amazing perfume. What are the conditions?'

'Conditions? What do you mean?'

'Do I start in two years? Do I have to give you the ideas and someone else creates it? Is it short-term and then you are done with me?'

Pierre sat next to her. 'Is that what you think?'

'I've been made lots of promises before. No one has ever taken me seriously...'

His gut twisted. 'I take you seriously. I think you are a better creator than me. And no one is a more skilled perfume maker than me.'

She laughed and the mood lightened. 'Do you only want me for my perfume skills?'

Her smile was coquettish and the room became electric. Daring to believe she was warming to the idea, Pierre stumbled for a response.

'Can there be one condition?'

Beginning to worry, his brow furrowed. 'What would that be?'

'That you come with the job?' It was his turn to be quiet. She filled the void.

'I arrived in Grasse having been dumped with a broken heart and sworn off love. All I wanted was to be a perfumer. To do something for me. Learn the trade, the skills and make beautiful perfume that women all over the world wanted to wear. But then I couldn't get into the official school, and the serious students at my accommodation, with their degrees and qualifications, thought I was a joke. Others in town also thought I was not worth consideration. But you were different, Pierre. Only you. You only laughed at me once,' he held up his hand in defence. 'And let me pick your precious flowers and work in your private lab.

'I've learned a lot since arriving, not only about perfume. I've learned that love comes in many forms and means something different to everyone.' Kitty paused. 'Stuart arrived yesterday, my ex-fiancé.'

'Wait, what, he's here in Grasse?' His body deflated.

'Yes, he came ...' Pierre held his breath. 'To tell me he's gay.'

'Gay?' Pierre felt both shocked and elated.

'Yes, you know, a homosexual.'

'Yes, I understand,' he laughed. 'I'm just surprised. That is the last thing I expected you to say.'

'He's in love and has married his sweetheart. And Pierre, he's so happy and deeply in love. So, it wasn't me. It was never going to be me. I understand that now, and it hurts less.'

Pierre nodded, deep relief coursing through his veins.

'I realised I was searching for the wrong thing. True love, real love, is when someone is prepared to sacrifice for another person and makes that person better by simply being in their life, being with them to buoy them and help them grow and develop. I was looking for some sort of Disney romantic love, but real love, it's so much more than that.' She gulped, gaining the momentum to continue. 'I never realised what love is really having grown up in a family that didn't love each other. I learned from the T.V. And I was so desperate to find it, not be like my parents. I think I wrapped myself up in a relationship at the first opportunity. I was blind and didn't understand it wasn't real.'

Pierre took the chance to jump in, needing to speak and

express himself. 'I've learned a lot, too. Kitty, I was scared. Scared of loving you, me not being enough, you not being safe…We're a right pair, you and I. Both of us are the products of sad family lives while also being very privileged and lucky in other ways.'

Kitty placed her hand on his and continued. 'And that is what you've taught me.' You've sacrificed and given me what I've wanted and unselfishly, for me, not for your own agenda but for me. That's pretty special and unique.' Her voice lowered, and she dipped her head, 'I think that's love. And I've learned too, that you give a lot to other people to atone for what you perceive to be your mistakes. You give and give and give, but don't seek anything in return. You deserve to be treated how you treat others. You are kind, considerate and have so much love. Pierre, you are not responsible for your brother's death. You never were, and you need to realise that and allow yourself to be happy. To let people love you back.'

To avoid tears springing to his eyes, he jumped out of his seat and reached for Kitty, pulled her to her feet and kissed her. There was no lead in, sweet touching along her jaw, or around her eyes, or neck. Instead, he covered his mouth with hers, with the passion that surged through him, for this woman. For the first woman to penetrate his veneer, crumble his defences. See right through him. Her lips were warm and moist and they welcomed him. Mixed in with the desire flooding through his body was hope and excitement, feelings he had not experienced for a long time. Emotions he had extinguished.

And Kitty Landers, an exotic Australian girl, was the reason. Who'd had her heart broken but had never truly shut herself off from love. Had always, even if she hadn't realised, been worthy of it, craved it, looked for it. Was he capable of being loved by her? His only doubt was if he could love her enough. It made his body ache with longing.

They pulled apart. 'Henri asked me to marry him.' Their foreheads rested against each other, but Pierre yanked his head back.

'Don't worry,' she jumped in, 'I'm not going to marry him, nor work in his shop or be part of a family that doesn't value the important and good work of women simply because they are women.'

His heart rate slowed. 'Noted,' he said with a grin. 'I would not have expected anything less.'

'I actually deliberated after he asked me though, thinking it was wise, the right thing to do, a sensible choice. Remembering, I thought true love wasn't possible. Until I saw him with another woman, and I didn't care; it had no effect on me. And then faced with Stuart, I didn't care either.' She reached for his hands again. 'But if you were with another woman, I would care a lot. My heart would shatter all over again, and I'd be devastated. You make me melt when you look at me with those eyes. The way you care for me. Your kindness to the children and to Mrs Roubillard makes me swell with pride. When I'm away from you, I can't stop thinking about you, and I ache to be close to you again. But more than any of those feelings, I know that you'll have my back always and we can be those people that lift each other up and help one another to be the best they can.'

This time, he trailed his fingers along her face, down her cheeks, along her chin, and traced her parted mouth before bringing his lips to hers.

'Thank you,' he whispered and then repeated it. 'Does this

mean you'll work in the company?' He did not say, 'Work for me' because they would be a formidable team.

She flung her arms around his neck and dropped kisses all over his face. 'Yes! As long as you can be by my side. I want to be the best perfumer Grasse has ever had, but with you by my side.'

'I can't think of anything I want more. I love you Kitty Landers,' and the words rolled off his tongue, sweet tasting and delicious. With her, he could forgive himself.

Chapter Twenty

Twelve months later

Kitty stood and stretched her aching back as strong hands circled her from behind and commenced massaging her sore spots. Her body curled in on itself in response before her long blonde tresses were swept aside, and warm and moist kisses landed on her neck. Pierre cradled her as they stood amongst the glorious colour-filled fields of centifolia roses during May harvest.

'This is going to be our best year yet,' he whispered in her ear, sending shivers racing up her spine.

She twirled on the spot to face him, her picking apron separating their bodies. 'It sure is,' she replied claiming his lips, tender and light as the soft and gentle breeze that blew through the fields.

'I want to kiss you all day,' he said, his breath hot against her face.

'Later,' she whispered against his lips. Kitty knew her eyes were smouldering.

Their love had been a slow burn. Pierre had given her the space to create and learn to trust him, learn her trade and revel in her passion: to be Kitty Landers without belonging to anyone. To become a perfumer.

She'd given him time to accept that she wasn't leaving him or Grasse, her sentiments were real, and she loved him despite the past and what he perceived as his mistakes. Kitty had been wrong about his philandering ways but the women of Grasse were nonetheless devastated at their union. The most rich and eligible bachelor in town was off the market and many hearts were broken that year; but not Kitty's.

'Refreshments for the love birds,' trilled Mrs Roubillard as she poured fresh lemonade from her pitcher with the help of Andreas. Kitty and Pierre pulled apart, their fingers lingering and stroking until they could no longer reach. Kitty felt the loss of his touch keenly.

'Thank you.' The perspiration settled on Kitty's skin after hours in the field. Andreas collected her empty glass. He, too, like her, had become a permanent fixture at the house after the tragic death of his wife. Mrs Roubillard would deny it, but Kitty would say she'd never seen the housekeeper happier. The French might think they were free ranging with love, but were they really? Kitty would argue the alternative. Pierre had tried to convince them to retire and enjoy the quiet solitude of their remaining years, but she'd have none of it, insisting her home was here with him and now Kitty.

Claude raced past the head of the row, and Marie stopped him for a cold drink, which he happily accepted.

Kitty had been right about one thing; love did take many forms. When she'd fled to Grasse devasted at the loss of the life she'd created in Australia, she could never have imagined she'd become the stepmother to ten-year-old boy who she would love unconditionally, as her own. Like any child, but especially one left orphaned, Claude needed to know he was loved and safe and secure, that he had a permanent home. Pierre needed to know he was loveable and loved, too. But her affection for Claude was something new and unique. With him, it was about what she could offer the damaged boy who'd known no parents or a stable home. And provided with those things in spades, he'd blossomed like their roses.

What had provided even greater joy was the burgeoning relationship that had developed between Pierre and Claude. Always close, their bond had deepened to mutual devotion over the last twelve months. Excepting when he attended the local school — Pierre was never going to send him away to an exclusive boarding school—the two were inseparable, and it appeared as if Claude might share the family gift of being *le nez*.

The remainder of the children at Rose House paused to accept drinks from Andreas, their little faces sweaty and their chests heaving from the games. Occasionally, they'd pick a blossoming bud and place it into the nearest pickers apron, but the premise of flower picking was soon overtaken by fun and frivolity. Kitty giggled as the children grasped both Pierre's and Claude's hands to rush them away into a game of chasey. Pierre took his flowers seriously, but the children always came first.

The children visiting from Rose House was her favourite day of harvest. Most of the picking occurred before the children arrived, but their squeals of joy echoed around the fields until

Mrs Roubillard served her famous feast for lunch. To add to the joy, there was no sign of the unseasonal rains yet this year. Today they stood under a clear, cloudless sky on a warm spring day. Perfect. Well, her version of perfect, anyway.

After the seasonal team of pickers had enjoyed their refreshments, Marie and Andreas walked back towards the house—the house where she now lived. Kitty pinched herself to make sure she wasn't dreaming, but the ache in her back told her she was alive, and she stood in the flower fields of Grasse.

Oh, how her life had changed.

Louisa, an eight-year-old quiet and shy girl who came to live at the home during the year raced past as fast as her little legs would carry her. Kitty reached out and grabbed her in a spontaneous cuddle. The shock caused the little girl to shriek before breaking into a fit of laughter.

The regulations and demographic of the home had changed, but Pierre and Kitty would provide a home to any child that needed it. Louisa and Kitty had become the best of friends and she often spent hours drawing in the corner of the lab while Kitty worked on her latest creation. Part of Kitty hoped that the girl wouldn't be adopted and could come and live with them too. Like Pierre, she wanted to bestow love upon every child that needed it.

Ms Dubois took over as leader of the chasey game and Pierre returned to picking. Neither of them needed to be harvesting, they had pickers for that and plenty of volunteers, but both refused to miss it. It would always be the most elemental process of perfume making, and Kitty never wanted to forget how she made perfume. Or stop enjoying the most delicious scent the centifolia released at this time of year, right before they were plucked. Pierre's passion was different. He loved every plant, those new to the ground and those he'd nurtured for years. He'd expanded the farm more recently, adding new fields and crops and spending less time in the workshop. He had Kitty for that. She spent her time creating and, when not creating, thinking about her next perfume. An additional perfumer had allowed Pierre to spend more time cultivating the farm and the essence of the very perfumes Kitty created.

With his help she'd developed the first of her series of fragrances, an ode to her homeland. There were four so far and she thought there might be two more to add to the collection. *Pacific Ocean Blue*, her very first was the most successful. It evoked holidays at the beach, relaxing weekends, and fun. *Eucalypt Forest Bloom* was as different to her first as the distance between the ocean and the forest. It was campfires and long walks in the heart of the bush. *Desert Orange Hues* transported the wearer to the wild, savage lands of central Australia and evoked aromas specific to that area. *Sunset Range Aurora* captured that summer feeling as a child growing up with mangoes, nectarines, watermelon and the heat of an Australian summer.

Kitty Landers had achieved her dream. She was a perfumer for one of the most successful perfume houses in the world. She had made her life in Grasse, southern France. Her student friends had graduated with honours from the prestigious perfume school and were experts on the chemical equations necessary for a wonderful perfume. Each had travelled home to hone their skills. None were currently employed at perfume houses.

A shout of *bonjour* rang out from the terrace signalling the arrival of Adrienne and Raph. Beside them Pierre's parents arrived and waved in greeting before they were bowled over by the barrage of children running in from the field. His father had survived his illness, and the rift between him and Pierre was healing. Kitty thought it was the power of the children and the love the children offered. His mother was often at *Maison de Roses*, and she was much happier and fulfilled. The hole in her heart was not as evident.

As their guests had arrived it was time to finish picking for the day and enjoy the feast of celebration.

Of life, of love and perfume.

Pierre was beside her in an instant and together, arms around one another, they walked to lunch.

Acknowledgments

I'm so excited to launch the second book in this series! And am so happy that you, dear readers, enjoyed the first. So much of the feedback was about being transported to the glitz and glamour of these rich and exotic worlds. I couldn't have asked for a better response as that is exactly what I wanted. So happy that I was able to achieve that and I hope there is the same experience with Kitty, Pierre and Henri in France.

Thank you as always to my early readers, Leigh and Lucy, such valuable feedback and it wouldn't be the same book without your input. To Annie Seaton for her valuable editing, Blurbs by Bel for making the blurb shine, Emma Powell of EJP Covers for the stunning cover.

And best news of all, next time I'll take you to the shores of beautiful Hallstat in Austria, and Switzerland. Happy reading!

About the Author

Leanne Lovegrove is a lawyer, wife and mother and a lover of romance and reading. Her law career created an addiction to coffee but provides countless story ideas. She is the author of romantic fiction. Leanne writes sweeping love stories with happily-ever-afters with strong female heroines and often set in the beautiful landscape of Australia. This is her second book in her European Tycoon series. This time she has left the shores of Australia behind for the exotic climes of various European cities for romances with dashing Tycoons. She lives in Brisbane, Australia with her husband and three children.

Other books in the European Tycoon series

The Spanish Jeweller (European Tycoons #1)
https://mybook.to/spanishjeweller

The Swiss Chocolatier (European Tycoons #3)
Available for pre-order

The Italian Winemaker (European Tycoons #4)
Coming soon!

To find out more about Leanne's books, you can find her here:

Leanne's website: www.leannelovegroveauthor.com

OR

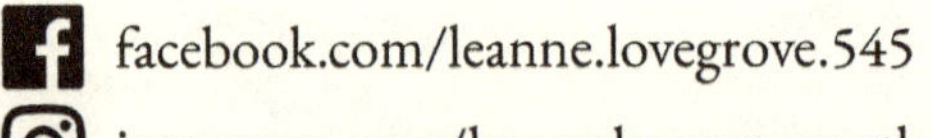

facebook.com/leanne.lovegrove.545

instagram.com/leannelovegroveauthor

bookbub.com/profile/leanne-lovegrove

Also by Leanne Lovegrove

Leanne's other novels:

Unexpected Delivery

Illegal Love

Keeper of the Light

A Good Life

Her Outback Home

Bellethorpe Series:

Love In Between (novella #1)

Caught In Between (novella #2)

Bellethorpe In Between Boxset (novellas #1 and #2)

Buried In Between novel #4

Novellas

Escapades of a Personal Stylist

Love on the Sweeping Plains

Anthologies

Love in a Sunburnt Land Vol 1

Love in a Sunburnt Land Vol 2

www.ingramcontent.com/pod-product-compliance
Lightning Source LLC
Chambersburg PA
CBHW020510120726

47904CB00003B/778